Tales of Tangier

Tales of Tangier

The Complete Short Stories of
MOHAMED CHOUKRI

Translated from the Arabic by
Jonas Elbousty

Foreword by Roger Allen

A MARGELLOS
WORLD REPUBLIC OF LETTERS BOOK

Yale UNIVERSITY PRESS | NEW HAVEN & LONDON

The Margellos World Republic of Letters is dedicated to making literary works from around the globe available in English through translation. It brings to the English-speaking world the work of leading poets, novelists, essayists, philosophers, and playwrights from Europe, Latin America, Africa, Asia, and the Middle East to stimulate international discourse and creative exchange.

English translation copyright © 2023 by Jonas Elbousty. The stories in this collection were originally published in Arabic as *Majnūn al-Ward* [*Flower Crazy*] © 1979 by Mohamed Choukri, and *Al-Khayma* [*The Tent*] © 1985 by Mohamed Choukri.

All rights reserved.

This book may not be reproduced, in whole or in part, including illustrations, in any form (beyond that copying permitted by Sections 107 and 108 of the U.S. Copyright Law and except by reviewers for the public press), without written permission from the publishers.

Yale University Press books may be purchased in quantity for educational, business, or promotional use. For information, please e-mail sales.press@yale.edu (U.S. office) or sales@yaleup.co.uk (U.K. office).

Set in Source Serif type by Motto Publishing Services. Printed in the United States of America.

Library of Congress Control Number: 2022941456
ISBN 978-0-300-25135-7 (paper : alk. paper)

A catalogue record for this book is available from the British Library.

This paper meets the requirements of ANSI/NISO Z39.48-1992 (Permanence of Paper).

10 9 8 7 6 5 4 3 2 1

To the memory of my father, my first teacher and mentor, who instilled in me the love of reading.—J.E.

Contents

THE TENT

Foreword

ROGER ALLEN

From a very young age, Mohamed Choukri, the Moroccan author of these stories, spent his life on the streets of Tangier, only learning to read at the age of twenty, while in jail. Illiteracy brings with it numerous developmental and social drawbacks, but one particular trait that it inevitably stimulates is that of memory. Once when I was attending a conference in the city, I accepted Choukri's invitation to have a drink in a local bar. As I was getting ready to return to my hotel, he asked me for my address. I began to search for a piece of paper, but he stopped me. "Just tell me your address," he said. I gave it to him orally and must assume that it was then stored away in his capacious memory along with a host of other information. At still another conference, this time in Toledo, Spain (where he gave a talk in perfectly idiomatic Spanish), he seemed to have recalled an earlier mention of my alternate career as a musician and insisted that we sit at lunch and discuss the merits of Beethoven's symphonies. The street urchin, dock porter, and precocious smuggler of former times had clearly used his acquired reading skill to the fullest, and yet, all that notwithstanding, vestiges of the spontaneity of the oral dimension were to remain a central component of his narrative creativity.

Much has been written (by Choukri himself, among others) about the origins and publication history of his most famous work, *For Bread Alone,* originally published in English in 1973 by Paul Bowles, and apparently based on Bowles's translation of Choukri's own oral performances of the narrative. In the book, Choukri, as a young boy, is forced to flee his family's household in order to escape the hideous cruelty of his father: the work opens with a description of his father breaking his baby brother's neck. He spends his teenage years on the streets of Tangier, homeless, illiterate, and abused—in other words, radically displaced. Because he is involved in drugs, sex, and smuggling, it is almost inevitable that he will end up in prison. And it is there that he learns to read. In subsequent years and decades, he is to become one of Morocco's most famous, indeed most notorious, writers.

The contents of the autobiographical narrative, with their explicit references to drugs and sex, together with the circumstances surrounding its publication (its Arabic version, *Al-Khubz al-ḥāfi,* did not appear until 1982 and was widely banned), brought Choukri both the fame and the notoriety. He was to add two more segments to this work, both of them initially published in Arabic (*Zaman al-akhta'* or *Al-Shuttar,* 1992, and *Wujuh,* 1996). In addition to that autobiographical trilogy, he also published collections of shorter narratives. Two of those, *Majnūn al-Ward* (1979) and *Al-Khayma* (1985), are translated here as *Flower Crazy* and *The Tent,* respectively. It is, I would suggest, precisely the appalling circumstances recounted by Choukri in his autobiography, especially its first part, that are reflected in the extraordinary vividness and immediacy with which his narrators are able to recount the scenarios, events, and conversations depicted in the stories of these collections.

As a recognized literary genre, the short story has, like other narrative types, been subject to a good deal of theoretical analysis in Western scholarship. Its every aspect—structure, style, themes, and length or lack thereof—has been much discussed. In the context of these two collections of Choukri's stories, we are dealing with narratives that happen to be comparatively short, rather than with the kind of short stories represented in Western literary traditions by such "classic" figures as Edgar Allan Poe, Guy de Maupassant, and Nikolai Gogol, or, in the specific case of Arabic, Zakariya Tamir and Yusuf Idris. True to his own background and storytelling instincts, Choukri offers his readers narratives that are at once colorful local vignettes and profound reflections on the lives and sufferings of his fellow "Tangerines," most of them full of conversation and characterized by subtle and poignant depictions of place, time, and mood.

The first story in *Flower Crazy*, "Violence by the Shore," sets a structural pattern that is to be repeated with variations in many of the subsequent stories in the two collections. A lively conversation in a café between a first-person narrator and an apparently annoying indigent is followed by a narrative switch in which we enter the consciousness of the latter figure as he makes his way to the beach, observes the people (especially the women) sunbathing and swimming, and plunges into the water himself.

The settings of these narratives reflect the physical aspects of their author's native city—its streets, markets, cafés, beaches, and fishing boats—and provide insights into the difficult and often suspect livelihoods of many of its poorest inhabitants. As a direct reflection of Choukri's own background and sense of social identity, his stories are minimally concerned with recounting the experiences of the wealthier segments of Moroccan society. In the first collection presented here, nothing better encapsulates the grotesque differences in social levels than its title story, "Flower Crazy," in which separate narrations are invoked to move between abject poverty with its accompanying miseries and the more visible public world of the modern metropolis.

The streets and markets of Choukri's fictional Tangier are places where newborn babies are for sale, children march with caged animals, and bars and cafés are filled with a cross section of people, many of them malcontent and downtrodden. Where else but in Choukri's imagination, one might ask, would one expect to encounter as complex a character as Bashir, with his ultimate decline and fall? The story "Talking About Flies Is Banned" even broaches a scenario close to Choukri's own life, recounting, through brutal conversation, the frightening experience of a falsely accused prisoner, while "The Poets," with its government repression, would seem to convey the author's reflections on the status of literature in his own country. Alongside stories in which characters converse or the narrator addresses his readers in the first person, are examples—"The Net," for example, and "Vomit"—that illustrate Choukri's remarkable ability to depict a situation through the power of unmediated and often brutally vivid description.

The title story of the second collection, *The Tent*, opens with the narrator describing an environment and set of characters that epitomize the circumstances at the heart of

Choukri's stories: as the text tells us, "The people left behind live outside their time, killing themselves bit by bit, following their predecessors—either killing or being killed." The narrator is eager to escape his usual environment and joins his friend on a ride to Monopolio, a notorious quarter of the city. We discover that the "tents" of the title are those usually set up for wedding ceremonies, although it is clear from the narrator's account that in this particular area of the metropolis they are also used for other kinds of encounter. As if to underline that, the story finishes with a rush to the sea, where the narrator describes in disarmingly explicit detail his sexual encounter with a woman who has left the tents with him and become his swimming companion.

As with *Flower Crazy*, the majority of the stories in *The Tent* involve a narrator who is intimate with Tangier—its streets, bars, restaurants, and markets. He feels at one with the inhabitants of this most cosmopolitan of Moroccan cities, as they struggle, often desperately, to earn and maintain a livelihood. In "The Spiderweb," a downtrodden shoemaker from the Atlantic coast town of Larache is brutally kicked and killed near a restaurant in a city square while the local lunatic laughs hysterically. In "Upright Crawlers," the narrator wanders through the city streets and encounters a wide array of townsfolk, among them a sickly old woman who begs him for some of his chewing gum, too weak even to stand in line and use the coin he has given her to purchase some for herself. "Widows 1" and "Widows 2" introduce readers to a desperate mother of two young girls; their father is no longer with them, and she is now forced to contemplate their dismal future while dragging the tearful girls away from the seashore.

One of the stories in this second collection takes readers away from Tangier and into the Atlas Mountains, to the town of Azrou. In a typical sequence of encounters with local people in a very different climatic region, the conversations of Choukri's narrator bring to the fore the harsh circumstances in which they live their daily lives, some of them, for example, without access to water. This guided tour of "this useless region of Morocco," as one character callously describes it, includes a visit to Ifrane, a Swiss-style chalet town, before coming to an end in a cold bar in Imouzzar filled with local prostitutes. An even less familiar, indeed maximally symbolic, setting is the site for "The Miniature Paradise," with its opening maxim "I do not think; therefore I am." God, the narrator explains, is ordering the expulsion of two people from "Paradise"—a woman first, then a man—because they think, dream, and feel sad. The conversations that each of them has with the guard supervising their departure are interspersed with a series of short, almost staccato, statements explaining exactly what it is that they have done to justify their expulsion. Thus ejected from this "Paradise," the two encounter each other, hold hands, and leave in search of "a new Paradise, one with no day and no night, no God and no guard."

As noted earlier, a major aspect of Choukri's storytelling artistry involves the sheer immediacy of its impact. In many if not most cases, readers are placed without any preliminaries into a conversation, one that involves a narrator, who may use the first or third person, sometimes interchangeably, and introduce one or more other characters. The setting is usually a public one, and the specific location and details will frequently be revealed only gradually. Discussion, disagreement, persuasion, oppression, and hatred—all are elements in the plethora of conversations that make up a sizable component of these stories. When a place, person, or mood is described, it is often done in brief phrases and sentences, unadorned by imagery or other literary devices. Readers are confronted with life as it is, without gloss, hyperbole, or sentiment.

So, dear reader, you are now invited to visit Choukri's Tangier, a city at the northwestern tip of Africa, washed by the breezes of both the Atlantic and Mediterranean, with the coast of southern Spain clearly visible in the distance. His unique knowledge of every aspect of Tangerine life, its people and its culture, makes him a singular guide, and his unrivaled ability to portray characters, situations, and moods gives each one of the stories gathered in this collection an authentic flavor and impact. That is the great gift to those who choose to enter Choukri's narrative world.

Flower Crazy

Flower Drift

Violence by the Shore

I felt relaxed as I sat in the comfortable Café Central, ignoring passersby. I was feeling calm.

"Anyone who wants to catch your attention," a friend once told me, "must shake you by the shoulder."

As the waiter handed me a cup of tea, I was enjoying the sun on my legs.

"He's roaming around. Pay no attention to him," he warned me. "He'll ask for a sip of tea. If nobody gives him a sip, he'll ask for the mint to suck on when he sees that the cup is empty."

"Who are you talking about?"

"Don't you see him? Maimoun."

I followed the waiter's gaze. Maimoun was leaning against the wall of Hotel Becerra.

"I didn't notice him."

"He always bothers the customers when it's my shift," the waiter added peevishly.

"You forgot to bring me an empty cup," I reminded him. I usually strain my tea into a second cup while I think. The waiter shook his head and walked off, seemingly with reluctance.

"That detestable person," Maimoun spat. "He curses me. I know what I'm going to do to all these waiters. I wish you could be here to see . . . This is how I'm going to attack them." He pantomimed unsheathing a dagger and stabbed wildly at the air. "None of them will escape me . . . After that, I don't care if I disappear from here. I'll leave this square to them."

A few passersby stopped, but then promptly continued walking, shaking their heads. Two children stayed, making fun of Maimoun.

I paused. "Stay away from them, Maimoun," I said gently.

"Bombs, green bombs! The knife and blood. Dead people. Living-dead people."

I took my cigarettes out of my pocket and offered him one. He came over and grabbed one, his dirty hand trembling. When the waiter reappeared, Maimoun nervously hopped back to the place he had been standing before. The waiter put down the empty cup, shooting a look at Maimoun.

"Maimoun will sit with me and drink tea," I told him.

"It's up to you," he replied, "but the owner doesn't tolerate this crazy man sitting in his café. When he stays around, he ends up fighting with someone. You don't know what he says when he talks to people."

"He's not going to bother anyone today. I guarantee it."

He shot Maimoun another quick glance. "I'm just warning you," he said. "You're responsible if anything bad happens."

I looked at Maimoun—he was smoking obsessively—and smiled at him as he gave the waiter a bitter look.

"I'll take responsibility," I told the waiter. "Nothing bad will happen." Though I did feel a bit nervous, thinking I might be held accountable for this man's behavior.

So, I thought, Maimoun has become this frightening and despised man. He used to be a guide, talking to tourists in many languages—one of the best guides in Tangier, in fact, fluent in English. That's what I had heard about him. Once I overheard him talking about his adventures in Italy, Portugal, and Spain. He was polite. He had an Australian girlfriend. The last time I'd seen him, he was working in a traditional crafts shop. He started scaring tourists with his nervous voice, though, and the store owner fired him. He made them feel unsettled, and they rushed out of the store without buying anything. That's what his boss said.

I looked at him. "Maimoun?"

"Yes."

"Come here."

The butt of his cigarette was turning to ash between his yellow fingers.

"Here I am."

"Sit." I pushed a chair toward him.

He lost his temper as he sat down. "Are you happy that the waiter humiliates me?"

"No."

"I'm going to wring his neck, like this!" Maimoun said, clenching his fists and making a twisting motion with his hands. "Or I'll throw my green bombs in his face."

"None of that's going to happen. No one here will humiliate you if you don't bring it on yourself."

I poured tea into the empty cup. His eyes sparkled. He moved his chair back and stood up.

"I keep my medication behind the hotel door."

A big smile formed on his face, his features tense. I was surprised: medication! His bare feet were muddy. His pants were torn at the thigh tops, his shirt was faded. He came back swatting at the air with a bunch of watercress.

"Wild mint," I whispered to myself.

"This watercress cures me," he said.

"What does it cure?"

"It cures me."

"What does it cure you of?"

"Nothing. It expels the illness from my body."

"So you're ill?"

"No. It protects me against illness."

I know that this bitter watercress is considered a kind of folk medicine. It is cooked with raisins and barley, then drunk on an empty stomach. Some people believe that it cures tuberculosis and other illnesses. Maimoun began plucking the small leaves and placing them carefully in his cup. He offered me a few bits. When he insisted, I covered my cup with my palm and smiled at him.

"No, Maimoun, not this time. When I get sick, I'll ask you to bring me this medicine."

"But it will protect you from illness now. It cures all illnesses."

"I'm not sick right now, Maimoun."

He gazed at his index finger as if consulting it, then stuck it in the cup.

A spoonful of flesh and blood, I thought.

He pushed the leaves vigorously to the bottom of the cup, then sucked his finger. He mumbled words I did not understand. I did not want to object to anything he did. He sipped with audible slurps. I felt the flow of warm, sweet liquid filling my own mouth, a mixture of honey and butter.

"And who's in paradise now?" he asked me, his eyes sparkling.

I should not put out that flame in his eyes, I thought. "You alone, Maimoun."

"And you?"

"Me?"

"Yes, you."

"Oh! Oh my God! You see . . . I'm here . . . "

He chuckled into his cup, which had filled with steam. His forehead was covered in sweat. The drops gathered in his sideburns, along the sides of his eyebrows, and at the base of his nose. His features hardened, then relaxed. I started counting the drips: one, two, three, four . . .

"Tell me, Maimoun, why don't you work anymore?"

He frowned. It was as if splinters were piercing my face. I felt a pain in my eyes, as when one leaves darkness and faces the sun. My stomach fluttered. Still I smiled at him as I waited for his response. He looked at me with fear on his face. To ease my anxiety, I reached for my cigarettes on the table. He grabbed my hand roughly and smiled back at me, nervous and shy, then clenched his teeth. The fluttering in my stomach subsided.

"Me? I won't smoke any of your fine cigarettes."

I was puzzled. "I just wanted to offer you another, Maimoun."

"Ha, you're a kind man. You're very kind to me, ha ha!" His laughter was agitated. "You're very kind to me; you're my brother." He paused, then asked: "Your name . . . ?"

"Sami."

"Ha ha! You're my brother, Sami! Aren't you my brother?"

"Yes, I'm your brother."

"You're just like me. Aren't you like me?"

"Yes, I'm like you."

"You are me, and I am you. Isn't that so?"

"Yes, it's so."

"You shouldn't be like the others, Sami," he continued. "You should be the way you are with me now, and I am with you."

A man stopped to make fun of him. Another man came to him and grabbed him by the sleeve. They moved on.

"Do you want to see that man's blood shed here, in the square?" Maimoun asked me with a sad look. "The firemen will come and wash the ground."

"No, no, Maimoun. Leave the square clean. Blood will pollute it, and pollute you as well. I don't want it to be polluted by anyone's blood."

"I'm like this, Sami. I want to see the blood of whoever annoys me shed on the ground," he continued, "and them thrashing like the sacrificed lamb on the Day of the Feast. When I take revenge, I calm down."

"And me, do I annoy you?"

"Not yet. But you're to be my friend. You've got to lend me some money so I can emigrate to Australia."

I felt my stomach flutter again. "But I don't have money," I said gently. "I'm like you, Maimoun."

"I have to go to Australia. I won't stay here, and Joney is there," he said wildly.

He started sucking at the remains of his cup, worked up about Australia.

"Emigration, emigration, Sami. When a man loves a woman like Joney," he muttered.

"But why Australia, Maimoun?"

"Because she's there. I love her, and she's there."

"Who?"

"Joney. Don't you know Joney, who was with me?"

"No, I don't know her. But the distance . . . "

As he produced a torn passport, the rapid gesture interrupted me. Some of its pages were missing, and the passport photo was worn out.

"I can follow her. Do you see, Sami?" he repeated insistently.

"Of course you can. But it comes at a high price, Maimoun," I said. "Was Joney good to you?"

"I don't remember. But if she sees me following her," he added, "she can't ignore me. She told me once that I was the only one who knew how to give her pleasure."

I smiled at him. "Her happiness, then, involves sleeping with you."

"Yes. I'm her happiness."

He removed the leaves of watercress from the cup and sucked on them. I thought that he'd returned to his senses when he was talking about Joney. His mind was in Australia, though he was here. When he was talking about Australia, he knew what he was talking about. The past; Joney and the bitter watercress that he was eating now. Maimoun, Joney, and I would all turn into bitter herbs. The world of today was the watercress of tomorrow. We are shit, transformed into pellets by a line of rolling scarab beetles.

"Let's go to the sea, if you'd like." His teeth gleamed, though his mouth was still green, oozing the mush of wild mint.

"Why?"

"To make some sea salt and sell it before the sun sets."

"Not today, Maimoun."

He took the rest of the mint from the cup and chewed it calmly. "When then? When the sun sets?"

"The sun will rise again."

He stared at me as he chewed the wild mint, and I smiled

at him. His stare became fiery. He turned to face a grim man who now stood in front of us.

"Leave my café!" the man growled.

Maimoun jerked; I gestured to him to remain seated. "But he's composed now," I objected. "He isn't doing anything."

"I know him better than anyone. You don't know what it's like when he behaves irrationally," the man said angrily. "He'll throw things in anyone's face when the blood rushes to his head."

Maimoun was silent. Was it out of fear or respect? We exchanged puzzled, sad looks, then he got up and left. I saw him standing at the end of the square, anxious but uninterested in those around him. He concentrated his gaze on me. Maybe he was upset with me because I was here, and he was there. Perhaps he was telling himself, *He isn't like me,* and feeling the magnitude of his loneliness.

He took a small, worn map out of his pocket and opened it. Putting it on the ground, he made as if to step on it with his right foot, but folded it up again and put it back in his pocket. Then he took off his shirt and lay down on the doorstep of the old Spanish telegraph office, naked to the waist. His big brown chest glistened in the sun.

"He likes the sun," a man sitting behind me said. "One day he stood here and shouted, 'I'm the god of the sun and the sea, and of this square.'"

Two men stopped in front of him. Maimoun put on his shirt, then sat on the doorstep, shaking his head at them. They left him there. He laughed loudly.

I heard the café owner telling another old man all about Maimoun's misdeeds. "Maimoun carried the curse of his parents wherever he went," he said. "When Mr. Idris came once from the countryside to pay a visit, Maimoun mockingly repudiated him: 'I have to be born again to be your son! I'm not content with you being my father. I am now the father and son of myself: I'm Idris and Maimoun.' Do you see? No doubt his dad was very hurt . . . I knew this man. He was respectful, a pious man. From home to mosque, and from mosque to work. The man who has a son like Maimoun must ask God for forgiveness for such a catastrophe."

With that, the café owner disappeared.

Maimoun looked concerned. He started to approach, stopped, then took another step in my direction. What would he do now? In my imagination, one of the cups was breaking, its splinters piercing my face. He pulled the chair out from the table forcefully and turned it upside down. "Let the devil sit on this chair now."

The café owner saw him and came out, barking, "You're crazy, you're cursed! I'm going to exile you from the whole of Tangier!"

Maimoun clapped his butt with the palms of his hands, like a clown. "I don't give a damn, old man! I don't give a damn!" he yelled.

The café owner wanted to chase him, but a customer held him by the arm. "You see how he is! You have to be rational, since he's crazy," the customer said. "They're going to take him to the asylum any time now. It'll be for his benefit. But you don't have to be the cause of this . . . "

"He knows what he's doing. He is choosing to drive people crazy. He himself is crazy, and yet he's not crazy," the café owner replied.

He paused and then pointed at me.

"Today you were the one who let him cause problems,"

he said. "When he finds someone to condone his behavior, he reigns. He thinks he's the guardian of this square."

"You know how he is," I said in my own defense. "You shouldn't provoke his anxiety if he's just sitting calmly."

He didn't answer.

"Unemployment is the cause of this madness," one of the customers behind me said.

"No, I don't think so," an old man responded. "In our time there was more unemployment than today. Yet nobody was driven crazy because of it. It is dissatisfaction that is destroying people's nerves. Contentment is wisdom."

Maimoun stood up with a hop, like a champion preparing for a running race.

"Look, he's getting ready to race an imaginary competitor," the café owner said. "He's always the winner in this imaginary competition. He runs against himself."

Maimoun bent his right knee; he looked to his right, to his left, and behind. Then he started running as hard as he could. Passersby were caught by surprise, as were the café customers.

"Where are the guards? They should take him away. He's a mad, miserable being," somebody muttered, irritated and impatient, "and his actions get on our nerves."

Maimoun turned around without stopping. When he reached the doorstep of the telegraph office, he raised his hand in victory. A child approached Maimoun and asked to race with him. Maimoun bared his teeth, and the excited child gave him a wide smile. Maimoun kicked him hard in the butt. The child jumped away, howling, then cursed Maimoun and ran away. Maimoun repeated the race three times. The final time, someone offered him a sandwich. He sat on the doorstep, chewing peacefully.

People, sun, and sea. Naked, soft, reborn. They slide against each other. A mirage of lakes, touching, embracing. Maimoun lusted after those soft bodies, naked tanned people mingling like watercolors. The people today are soft, light, as they float in the sea.

He became angry with himself. He is gruff, and they are soft. The sun blinds him. The breeze in the air softens his blindness. He has lost himself enough for today, further estranged from people.

It has been a long time since I've seen anyone give me a tender look, he thought. They do not turn to me, unless I challenge them with angry looks. What consoles me is that they treat me with such caution.

The sand slides under his feet like silk pillows. It is as though I am walking on the bellies of frogs, he tells himself. He thought his whole body might melt. The echoes of melodies ring inside his head. His exhaustion gives him a pleasurable numbness. *No one is ever alone in this world.* Is that a lie as well? His demeanor reflects unease. Faces avoid his gaze. His looks terrify the bathers. He won't move from his spot. This makes him feel that he is victorious over anyone who might look at him askance, at least in his imagination. Their defeat pleases him. He clenches the sand in his fist, holds it tight: molten gold. He imagined his rage against certain people with this clenching of sand. "People are being molded in my fistful of sand. In my hand. Someday they will dry up, coming to resemble what I feel now within my body," he thought to himself.

> A tanned young girl comes out of the sea
> Her chest rises
> God is in the hearts
> She flows with agility
> God is in the waters and mirages
> Her eyes are blinking
> Two dying butterflies
> God is in the light and darkness
> She walks gracefully
> God and beauty are wherever we are.
> If I were a deity
> I would have given her eternal life.

His whole body jerked with both pleasure and anger. She looked at him, trembling, losing her elegance and grace. One bite of her body, and his drought would end. The snake of lust awoke, wild, in his eyes. The young woman, afraid, took refuge with a group of young men who were lying on the sand. The way they were stretched out reminded Maimoun of sardines being grilled. That only amplified his hunger and thirst. Their bodies were alluring. He picked up some shells and turned them over in his hand. Had they been jewels, he could have followed Joney. O God of good fortune! Make jewels of these seashells so that I may follow Joney! He entered a magical world, quietly grasping what was happening.

He adored looking at seashells on the shore of al-Hoceima. The sea breeze pierced his shirt, and he felt the flow of air under his armpits. He stopped dreaming. He saw a young man approaching and imagined him in a wild race with himself toward the sea. Maimoun got ready. The young man reached him. Maimoun flew like a rooster: shroop . . . shroop . . . shrooop . . . shrooooop . . . shrooooo000p. The young man in the water shuddered in amazement. Maimoun stayed underwater. He floated far away. He hit the water forcefully. He dived again. He swam like a sea dog. He moved ahead powerfully. He surfaced and stood up, panting like a fish out of water, exhausted, then came out, dripping. His clothes stuck to his body like melted wax—a statue made of plaster, not yet polished. He walked along the seashore. The fly of his pants revealed his shrunken snake between two hard figs. He threw himself on his stomach, leaning his head on his left arm and leaving the other extended. A severe headache shot through his right temple; a stabbing pain in his gut; a fatal drought in his body. He fell asleep. His exhausted breathing brushed away the spot of sand shaded by his face and arm. He was like a huge fish thrown up by the sea.

Sweat, dizziness, and anger. When he woke up, his clothes were burning. His head, his armpits, and the wrinkles of his stomach were soaked in sweat. He took off his shirt and felt a breeze. He walked toward the water. God is in the sea. His shirt dangled in his hand like a dead wild rabbit. He submerged his head and saw the little sand ripples forming. God is in the depths and on the surface. He felt a kind of sea rapture. He dove, hitting the water headfirst, like a dolphin. He felt weightless. His dizziness faded away. When he got out of the water, he walked and wandered, his shirt flowing in his hand. His body was stretched like a drum, his pants wrinkled. He sparkled. He was tired of thinking about people. Here I am, the way I want to live among you. He wished he could rejoice, for one anonymous birthday with other people, but he had lost that old feeling.

"We aren't better or worse than people . . . "

"Then what are we, mother?"

"Don't you know?"

"No."

"We're like that. We're the way you see, my son . . . "

"And what's that noise outside?"

"Don't talk like that. Don't you know that we're celebrating? We should be proud of our feasts."

"No, not like that," his father objected. "You know nothing about our feasts. Every feast is sins and carelessness in the street."

A human mass, far off, sparkled in the sun. He moved closer to this naked lust. The woman's head was wrapped in a towel. A living body ready for embalming. He looked back where he had been. The bathers were as small as dwarfs. A field of sand planted with humans. Their heads came together and then parted. The lust grew in his body. His shirt fell out of his hand. He became agitated and crazy. Shivers of pleasure overwhelmed his body. In his imagination, he was being whipped with wet branches. His head was spinning with sweet feelings. Nectar was flooding his dry mouth. A feminine scent, mixed with the smell of the sea, thrilled his nose. He had not touched a woman since Joney had left him. His hand shivered as it touched his aroused manhood. Joney! Joney! Here I see you. God does not turn seashells into jewels. God is in Australia, and he is here too. God is wherever we are. In his imagination, his snake was entering Joney's burrow. His nakedness grew rougher, violent. His eyes blinking in the sun, he cast his shadow over the body stretched on the sand. He no longer saw anything, only a light blonde from whom fell the imaginary mulberry leaf. He threw himself at her, violently. He pleasured himself loudly. In vain she hit at him and screamed. He was heavy on top of her. His nails were in her skin. Oh! How Joney loved it when he would tear off her clothes! The salt taste of her skin in his mouth blended with the blood from her scratches. He got up. He looked back at the line of dwarfs racing toward him. He spat on her. She gave him a look, pitiful and scared. He stared at the sea. An old longing for the sea surged out of him . . . He began to hurry. Running away . . . running away . . . running away . . . shroop, shroop, shrooop, shroooop, shrooooop. Blind, soft strokes. His clothes fell to the sand like a dead octopus. She stood up, shocked. The dwarfs became giants. Maimoun took refuge in the sea, which he worshipped. She frowned, completely silent.

The dwarfs—the giants—wondered to themselves:

"What does he plan to do?"

"He will get scared. Once he's swallowed some water, he'll back off. You'll see."

"We have to do something for him."

"Look at him. He's standing there as if he's in a well."

He plunged. A second later, he floated to the surface again.

"He's fainting."

He plunged again . . .

Tangier, 1977

The Net

To the child "Chakib Bouzid"

He walked along the beach from its start until he reached the point where fishing boats were hauled up away from the sea. Back and forth he went, four or five times. Each time he roamed a bit farther, expanding the scope of his search. He kept searching through the sand, including the spot frequented by beachgoers.

He found a plastic ring that did not fit any of his thin fingers. He put it in his pocket, hoping to sell it in the city. He often found plastic things on the beach and sold them to companions in his poor neighborhood.

He found a pacifier and washed it in seawater. He felt like putting it in his mouth to suck on.

Every day his mother went to the Grand Socco. She would stand and wait for hours with other female domestic workers until someone would come and take one of them to work at his house. When the boy came back, if he found his mother still waiting, she would sometimes give him a pita with oil and sugar inside.

A plastic sandal was half buried in the sand. His heart skipped a beat, and his eyes widened joyfully. He put the pacifier in the pocket of his patched pants, then wiped the sand off the sandal. It was white and still in good shape. He kept searching around the spot, using his bare feet at times, then digging with his hands. The hole grew longer and wider. The sun started making him feel dizzy. Sweat poured down his thin, pale face. His limbs were shaking. The toes of his feet hurt from kicking through the sand and hitting hard objects buried there.

He walked toward the sea and rinsed his face and limbs. A plastic mineral-water bottle bobbed amid the ebb and flow of the waves. He grabbed it. It was empty. He removed the cap. He peed in the bottle, then put the cap back on. He took a step back and drew a deep breath. He ran to the water's edge and threw the bottle as hard as he could. It sank briefly, then floated to the surface. His anger and exhaustion eased a bit.

He walked along the shore. Far from where he was, people were swimming or lying on the sand. It was the end of summer, and the end of visitors—those sea-loving foreigners.

It was all useless and torn stuff; nothing worth selling. Carrying the little sandal, he kept walking. He picked up a small plastic bucket. It had no handle and was split along the side. He put the sandal in it, then started meandering in various directions. Digging in the sand, looking for the other half of the sandal pair, had sapped all his energy. He had not eaten breakfast yet. He decided to cut short his search for lost things.

"People don't lose or forget things," his mother had once told him. "If they lose or forget something, it's something of no value; they throw away the things you find; they don't lose or forget them."

Trash that neither sold nor provided food. Worthless. But he could not find any other work; all he could do was go to the shore in summer, every morning and sometimes in the evening as well.

"When I grow up," he told his mother one day, "I'm going to be a fisherman just like my father."

His father had died young, drowned at sea with two others in a fishing boat that capsized.

A small plastic fish. He grasped it and examined it closely, then placed it carelessly in the bucket. That morning his hunger was making him lose interest in the little things that normally kept him entertained.

Fishermen put out the big net. Arching backward, they tugged on the rope until they almost fell down. Their motion looked like trees in a strong wind, bending over and then standing upright again. He looked at them with admiration, longing to join them and throw his strength into tugging on the rope, which kept splashing sprays of water as they heaved on it. What emerged from the sea distracted him from searching in the sand. Shiny fish jumped in and out of the net. Some of the fish slipped out of the net and fell back into the sea.

He threw the bucket down and began to help them gather the fish that had jumped out of the net. None of the fishermen objected to his working with them. They did not talk much. When one of them spoke, he would yell rather brusquely, then resume his silence just as swiftly as he had broken it. They bickered among themselves about the way the net was being tugged as they worked. He started helping them sort the fish. He felt he could work as skillfully as they did, catching and sorting the jumping fish. The large pile was shrinking, while the smaller piles were growing bigger and bigger. When fish wriggled in his hands and struggled to escape, he was spellbound. He liked the color of one small fish and put it aside. It was still jumping and wiggling.

One of the men gave him a few of the smallest fish. He took the fish he liked most and put it with the others. By then, the beautiful fish he liked was gradually losing its strength. He took it to the water and gently put it in. It started bobbing like a cork. He left it there, still unsteady as small waves toyed with it, then returned to his piles of fish.

He felt a bit sorry for the beautiful fish. He dug a hole and buried the sandal. He put the rest of the fish, along with the plastic fish, in the bucket. He started heading away from the shore. He paid no more attention to the sand, which was beginning to heat up under his feet. Such things no longer appealed to him. He looked at the fish in the bucket. Some of them were dying.

Near the pool, he noticed a sleeping cat. He grabbed the plastic fish and threw it to the cat. The cat shivered excitedly. It threw itself on the fish, smelled it, licked it, and flipped it over with its claws. The cat continued toying with the fish, its gaze darting back and forth between boy and fish. He then threw the cat a real fish. It abandoned the stiff fish, caught the live one, and took it back to the spot where it had been lying under the roof of the pool. Leaving the plastic fish where it was, he went on his way.

Tangier, 1977

The Ones Who Came Back

Early risers were picking up the red flyers that had been left on the road and front doorsteps. The flyers were written in Arabic, French, Spanish, and English.

They would stop, look around in every direction, and either run back to their homes or head out of the city. They would wake each other up, anxious and rough.

"Why are they going to bomb the city?" they asked, confused about the meaning of the notice. "Who's going to bomb it?"

The flyers made no sense, but the idea of leaving made perfect sense. They gathered, dispersed, consulted, cooperated, hurried, fainted. They left—some by car, others on foot. They ran and stumbled. They came out of their homes, then, hesitant to leave, went back, then came out again. Terror was contorting their faces and actions.

Many of them left in pajamas, barefoot and half naked. Women and young girls and children who were crying and wetting themselves. They headed for the mountains, the suburbs, the coasts. They clung to the backs of trucks. Three or four would ride on a single motorcycle. Most of them retreated to the mountains so that they could watch the bombing.

The only ones who stayed in the city were cripples, madmen, adventurers, and animals. They spent the entire day waiting for the city to be bombed. Near the coasts, the prices of fish and water were very high. They traded their clothes for fish and water. In the suburbs and on the Big Mountain, they raided the fruit orchards, vegetable gardens, and livestock pens. A bloody battle broke out over a stolen goat. Another group chased a shepherd with mud bricks and stones and seized several sheep from his flock. They climbed trees and rode animals and each other.

In the evening, they went back the way they had left. Many people fled in their cars to other cities. Some of them came back, others did not.

They ran. They collapsed in exhaustion. Traces of terror were still visible, and yet their determination to face their destiny appeared stronger in their eyes—stronger than fear.

They carried flowers, branches, batons, fruit, vegetables, livestock, and birds both dead and alive.

They found their city silent, quiet. Here and there, madmen and adventurers were walking around casually. Every now and then, madmen's laughter could be heard. They were talking loudly, pointing at the people who had come back, or at the void. To those who had returned, the flyers still made no sense, but to them their return seemed just as reasonable as their departure.

Tangier, 1971

Motherhood

"Are you sure she's serious?" the young woman asked me in the jewelers' quarter.

"I've known her well for many years," I said. "She wants to devote the rest of her life to raising a child. I've told her about you. Don't worry."

"Did you tell her about my work in the bar?"

"Of course. She had the same job when she was young."

We were walking slowly, heading toward the Petit Socco. Her face lit up, and she let out a chuckle.

"Anisa! What are you laughing at?"

"I'm not laughing at anything."

"You can't be laughing at nothing. Something's making you laugh. What is it?"

"You're right, something made me laugh," she said. "I forget what. Sometimes I imagine things that I can't name. Sometimes, by the time I'm done laughing about one thing, I've started laughing about something else."

From time to time, I glanced at her belly. Her pale face was small, beautiful, and childlike. As we reached the Petit Socco, some of the café customers looked at us. I knew a few of them. Her belly was not especially obvious. Yet she said she would be delivering within a week.

"We're getting close to her restaurant," I said as we approached Bareed Road.

"Do you think we'll find her there?"

"She either sleeps after lunch or chats with the waiters."

We found the restaurant empty. At the far end of the hall was a rectangular-shaped room furnished in Moroccan style. I knew that she was probably taking a nap or lying down as she pondered her problems. I greeted the cook, who nodded toward the room. I left Anisa standing in the hall and went into the dark room. The señora was taking a nap; she looked like a beached whale.

She woke up. "Who's there?"

"Señora Alicia, it's me, Botami. Are you asleep?"

She sat up, then stretched and yawned. "No, I'm not sleeping. I'm just having a little rest."

She was always complaining about something. That was how she entertained herself.

"I've brought her to you."

"Who?"

"The pregnant young woman I told you about."

"Oh! Where is she? Bring her in."

I turned on the light and called to Anisa. The wall was decorated with a large tapestry with an embroidered picture of a palace and two Arabian knights on horseback. A young girl sat with her arms around the waist of the first one, and his retainer was looking back toward the palace as his horse jumped over a flowing stream.

"Here she is," I told Señora Alicia in Spanish.

She examined her with a serpent's gaze. "Pretty."

"The father of the child is even more beautiful than the mother."

Anisa and I sat down on the Moroccan divan. The señora gave me a cigarette. Anisa refused, even though she was a heavy smoker. I lit both the señora's cigarette and mine.

"You can see his father if you want," I told the señora.

"I believe you."

"Señora Alicia is impressed by your beauty," I told Anisa, who did not know any Spanish.

"Thank you."

"I'm making a deal with her."

"Thank you."

"The father of the child is dark," I told the señora, "and the mother is blonde, as you can see. No doubt the child will be magnificent."

She drew on her cigarette.

"How old is she?" she asked.

"Twenty."

"And the father?"

"Twenty-one," I said, without consulting Anisa. "I know him well. He is a modern young man, the most handsome young Moroccan I've ever seen in Tangier."

"How much does she want?"

"She wants the cost of delivery in a good hospital and a small sum so that she can return to her hometown of Khenifra."

"Is she sure she'll deliver this week?"

"She's certain," I said. "She doesn't lie; she tells me everything. Believe me, Señora."

"She seems in good health."

"She is strong, Señora. She eats and sleeps well. And so does the father," I added. "He exercises. You can see him if you want. He spends time in Anthios Café."

"I haven't heard of that café."

"It's on the main street, a new café frequented by young men and women. It's very modern."

"You know I want a boy."

"I believe she'll deliver a boy."

"How do you know?"

"I don't know," I continued. "But I've a feeling she'll deliver a baby boy. She'd like a baby boy as well, even if she doesn't want to keep him."

I visited Anisa in the apartment of her friend Milouda and found her lying in bed, with her baby next to her. She threw a quick glance at the sleeping baby.

"What did you decide?"

"I'd rather sell myself than sell him."

"What should I tell her?"

"Come up with something."

I found Señora Alicia taking a nap in the same room as before. I sat down.

"She delivered a baby boy," I told her.

"Wonderful!" she said in relief. "She's lucky. Is she out of the hospital?"

"Yes. She's staying with a friend."

"How's her health?"

"Good. As though she'd not just had a baby."

"And the baby?"

"He's in good health as well. However, he's disappointed us."

"What's happened?"

"I'm sorry, but he's deformed."

"Are you kidding me?" she said, clearly upset.

"Believe me. He's deformed, Señora Alicia. His head is big and elongated; his eyes are as small as the eyes of a dead fish; his left eye is lazy. He has very short arms, six fingers on each hand; his legs . . . "

"Enough! Please, enough!" she interrupted me, her voice filled with both disgust and fear.

"I'm sorry."

She lit a cigarette and started smoking nervously. She did not offer me one, as she usually did. I lit up one of my own black cigarettes and pretended to be sorry.

"What about my money?" she asked after a moment's pause.

"I'm sorry, Señora Alicia. I'm very sorry. But there's still hope."

She didn't say anything.

"There are three or four other pregnant women who'd like to get rid of their newborns. They're also beautiful and very modern, all young and elegant."

"I've never seen a crook like you. Do you want me to pay one of them another seven hundred dirhams?"

"No. This time it won't be like that," I told her as she continued her nervous smoking.

"So?"

"You won't pay anything until you get the child you like. I know a girl who'll be delivering soon. She's more beautiful than the other one. Believe me, believe me just one last time. She's very pretty and very modern. We just hope that she'll have a baby boy."

"I swear to you that I've never seen a con artist like you."

"Believe me, Señora Alicia. I promise you that you'll receive the most beautiful child from one of these pregnant women."

Tangier, 1972

People Laughing,
People Sobbing

A beggar was holding his hand out. "Give me something, please," he said with a laugh.

Adil refused with a wave of his hand. People were laughing, staring at him as he stood there in the square. Guffaws came from the café, shops, streets, and balconies—everywhere.

Two men were fighting, laughing. Their faces were bleeding. Adil sat down. They gave him strange looks.

"What will you drink?" the waiter asked, laughing.

"Coffee."

The waiter looked at him, laughing. A woman and her child came to a stop, laughing. She shook the boy by the shoulder, laughing, "What are you saying? What are you saying?"

"You're crazy!" the child replied with a laugh, massaging his temple with his finger. "I didn't do that and didn't say anything."

She pinched his ear. He began to cry, laughing.

"This is what's left for you," she said, laughing. "Walk in front of me, you little bug. I know you well."

She pushed him ahead of her, laughing. The child walked in front of her, crying-laughing. An old man stopped laughing and fainted. They gathered around him. Adil heard them saying that he was sick.

"I know where his house is."

"Help me carry him."

They disappeared with him into the alleyway, laughing. The children memorized their lessons, laughing.

Their voices were louder than their teacher's:

I once had a nightingale
In a cage made of gold
Its feathers were gorgeous.
It was beautiful, with a long tail.

A fat woman came to a halt nearby, laughing heartily. She leaned her hand against the wall and lowered her head. She stopped laughing. They stared at her in astonishment. Some people stood near her laughing. She started laughing again, clutching her heart.

The waiter put down the black coffee, laughing. They were all amazed that Adil was silent and sad. He in turn was amazed by their weird mouths and their eyes, tearful with joy. He noticed that some of them were not laughing.

Perhaps the people who aren't laughing are new arrivals to the city, like me, he thought.

"Hello! Hello!" the handicraft vendor said with a laugh to a man and woman who were not laughing. "Here! Come on!"

"No, thank you," the man replied cheerfully.

The two walked on, now laughing. Adil noticed that the people who took a momentary break from laughter kept on smiling and having fun. Nearby, a giggling boy polished a man's shoe. His chuckles increased each time he looked at gloomy Adil. Adil was annoyed by the laughing boy's glances. When the boy was finished with the second shoe, he pointed to Adil's shoes. Adil refused, waving his hand and shaking his head.

"What's wrong with you?" the boy asked. "Are you sick?"

"No," Adil replied impatiently.

The boy was dismayed. He walked away, laughing.

"Enough laughing, please," the hotel owner said from the doorway. "Some people are still sleeping,"

Adil got up from his bed laughing. He went to the bathroom laughing.

"What's wrong with you?" the owner of the hotel asked, sobbing. "Are you sick?"

Adil didn't answer him. He could not stop himself from laughing. He went out laughing. In the cafés, shops, balconies, streets—everywhere, people were sobbing and grieving. They stared at him in amazement. He stood in the square, then sat down laughing.

"What will you have to drink?" asked the sobbing waiter.

"Black coffee," responded Adil, laughing.

The waiter walked away, sobbing. Adil kept laughing. His eyes were full of tears. They turned red and became swollen.

Old people were sobbing. Young people were crying and screaming. Their eyes were swollen, as they had been yesterday. Their expressions were stern, their features sad and pale.

He laughed and laughed. He did not know how to stop laughing. The waiter put down the black coffee, sobbing. He gave Adil an astonished look. Adil's laughter increased.

"What's wrong with you?" the waiter asked. "Are you sick?"

"No. I'm not," Adil replied.

As had happened the day before, some people were laughing.

Perhaps people who aren't laughing are new arrivals to the city like me, he thought.

The handicraft vendor, sobbing, called out to a man and woman who were not sobbing.

"Hello! Hello!" he said. "Come on! Here!"

"No, thank you," the man said cheerfully.

They walked on, laughing. The beggar stretched out his hand.

"Give me something, please," he begged.

Adil gave him half a dirham with a laugh. The shoeshine boy pointed at Adil's shoes, sobbing. Adil looked at his shoes, laughing, and waved him off, shaking his head. He gave the boy half a dirham. The boy walked away, sobbing sadly. They all gazed at him in astonishment. Their sadness and misery intensified, while Adil grew happier the more he laughed.

Adil noticed that for those people who stopped sobbing for a moment, sadness remained deeply ingrained in their expressions.

Tangier, 1971

Children Are Not
Always Stupid

The march started from one of the neighborhoods, with seven of them. Two carried a white sign with nothing written on it. At the front was a child carrying a white pigeon in a green cage. As they walked down each road, more children joined them. Some carried cages with birds. Many held cats, rabbits, roosters, and little chicks. Their dogs followed them. The march grew larger as they proceeded from one road to another. It became impossible to tell how many they were. They were utterly silent. Passersby smiled at them, but no one laughed. People wondered what the march was about. The animals they were carrying added to the mystery. The elders were clueless. Probably only the original seven children knew. The new children joining the march did not know. They did not speak, push, or rush. They kept walking down the ancient roads. Their numbers kept increasing. Their large group and serious silence astounded passersby. Those children, today they looked more intelligent than ever. That was what people said. Fathers and mothers walked behind or alongside the march. Other children joined in too; they would separate from their fathers and mothers and join the march. A child on the road was crying. He wanted to take part, but his frightened mother forbade it.

He kept kicking and crying. Biting her hands, he managed to get away from her and join the march, silent and calm. He did not even wipe away his tears so as not to disrupt the order of the march.

When they reached the small square, they stopped for a moment. Customers who were sitting in the cafés stood up respectfully. A large crowd gathered round them. People watched from the balconies of hotels and houses. The children were silent and solemn. They did not look around them; they only looked straight ahead. They were shaping a world of their own. Not a single child was seen outside the march.

"When children act in this mature way," an onlooker said to his friend, "their elders should treat them with respect. Indeed, the world seems to have a different significance."

The march moved forward. They arrived at the square, where they stopped and made a big circle. Three children moved toward the center of the circle. Two of the three raised the smallest child onto their shoulders. The little child took out a white piece of paper with nothing written on it. He gave a speech in silence, opening his mouth but not saying anything. They all looked at the small speaker, silently mouthing words. When he finished his silent speech, he folded the paper and put it back in his pocket. Children and grown-ups clapped. The two children put their little colleague down gently. The child with the white pigeon in the green cage stepped forward and released the pigeon into the air.

Other children released hundreds of sparrows and pigeons into the air, then released the other animals that did not fly. The audience clapped. Bedouin and city-dwelling women, wearing traditional gowns and veils, ululated. Every-

one was smiling and laughing. Automobile traffic stopped for
a few minutes. Not a single car horn was heard complaining
about the interruption. They all were watching sparrows and
pigeons flying in the sky, while the non-flying pets romped
safely between their legs. The children started to disperse,
shouting happily:

"Long live pigeons!"

"Long live sparrows!"

"Long live chickens!"

"Long live rabbits!"

"Long live cats!"

"Long live dogs!"

Fathers and mothers hugged and kissed their children.

Tangier, 1973

Shahrayar and Shahrazad

The phone rang three times. On the fourth ring, Shahrayar rubbed his eyes and picked up.

"Yes, who's speaking?"

"Shahrayar, good morning! Listen, we're waiting for you at Café Comedia."

"I'm sorry. I can't join you two."

"Why? What's happened?"

"Later. I'll tell you later."

"Are you ill?"

"I don't know."

"So, what's happened?"

He thought a moment. "I don't know," he said. "You'll find out later."

"You're acting strangely this morning. Listen . . . "

"What?"

"Take a walk around the Big Mountain. You'll find peace of mind."

"Okay. Thank you. I hope you two have a fun trip."

"Bye."

He put the phone down. Getting out of bed, he stretched, then headed for the bathroom. He looked in the mirror: the same face. He washed his face, but did not dry it with the towel. He felt the water dripping onto his chest. He went back to the bedroom. The same pictures: his mother Shahrazad, his aunt Shahrazad, his Spanish girlfriend Shahrazad, his sister Shahrazad with her friends the brunette Shahrazad and the blonde Shahrazad, and finally a picture of himself in his twenties.

He went out onto the terrace. As usual, he cast a glance toward Regnault High School then toward the sea, the Charaf plateau, and Goya Street. A girl came out on the balcony of the house next door. She started hanging up nightgowns. Her dress was long, her chestnut hair curly, her figure curvy, and her face shaped like a full moon.

"Are you the daughter of Mr. Shahrayar al-Hajjaj?"

"Yes."

"I know your father, and your mother Shahrazad as well."

She gave him a strange, fleeting glance. "You live here now?"

"We're only staying for the summer. You were still very young when I used to give private lessons to your brother, Shahrayar, and your sister, Shahrazad, at your house."

"When we were living in the Kasbah."

"Exactly. You were a baby and learning how to walk."

"I don't remember."

She finished hanging the clothes, then leaned her elbow on the balcony railing.

"What's your name?"

"Have you forgotten my name?" she replied, surprised.

"You were so little. You could walk, but you couldn't speak yet."

"My name is Shahrazad."

"And your age?"

"Sixteen."

"You've grown."

She gave him a smile, then disappeared. As usual, he glanced at Regnault High School, the sea, the Charaf plateau, and Goya Street.

He went inside and headed for the bathroom. He looked in the mirror: the same face, the water droplets now dried. He went into the bedroom. He glanced carefully at all the pictures, as usual. He thought about his strange feelings that morning, feelings that made him look at things more closely than usual.

He got up and went out onto the terrace. As usual, he directed his four glances in order. Shahrazad was there, wearing a different dress, one with green and orange stripes. This time her hair was loose, smooth and shiny. She leaned against the balcony railing and gazed up at the sky. He gazed at her full breasts; then he too gazed up at the sky. He couldn't remember the last time he'd looked at the sky.

He went back inside. Taking a cigarette out of the pack, he lit it, then put the pack and the box of matches in the pocket of his pajamas. He remembered: *I was eleven when I smoked my first cigarette. It was Eid al-Adha. I sat in Mr. Adlani's café and smoked my first cigarette. I drank green tea as well. It was in Tétouan, in 1946. But the sky—I remember neither my first look up at it nor the last time I looked, until Shahrazad, the daughter of Mr. al-Hajjaj, reminded me. Now some old forgotten sights are being revived amid strange feelings, along with some new ones that I am only beginning to discover.*

He went onto the terrace again. As usual, he directed his four glances in order, and then added the fifth, forgotten glance up to the sky. The sixth glance had disappeared.

Perhaps I looked at her longer than I should have. Perhaps she thought I was flirting. In fact, I did not feel any desire to flirt with her.

He went back inside and started to get dressed. It was Sunday. Where shall I go today? Should I take a walk to the Big Mountain as my friend, plump Shahrayar, suggested? In two hours' time they'll arrive, he and his friend Shahrayar the thin, in Ceuta. I don't know yet where I'll be in two hours time.

He went to the bathroom and combed his hair. Every time he checked his thick black hair, there was more white. He touched his face.

I won't shave this morning, he told himself.

"Why did you give up going to the beach?" I once asked my thin American friend, Shahrazad. "A suntan suits your face."

"Really? Thanks," she replied. "But for whom should I make my face beautiful? Should I beautify it for you?"

He went into the room and looked carefully at each photo. As usual, he took three books and went out onto the terrace. He directed the four glances in order, then added the fifth, forgotten glance up to the sky. The sixth glance was still hiding.

The big fat female dog was dragging the thin little girl. Shahrayar focused his gaze on the thin girl, then on the fat dog. The fat dog bared her teeth and lunged at Shahrayar the thin. The thin girl used her entire body to pull back.

"Luna!" she yelled. "Calm down! Calm down, Luna!"

Shahrayar stepped quickly backward and fled to the other sidewalk. He looked at the fat dog and thin girl. Panting and trembling, he picked up the book he had dropped. He looked all around him. There was nothing nearby he could use to hit the fat dog. He even considered hitting it with the book. But what would happen, he wondered, if it became more agitated and attacked him?

"Pardon, sir," the girl said. "She doesn't mean any harm."

If only I could get the thin girl to hit the fat dog, he thought.

He saw two young men approaching, laughing. One was fat, the other thin. His heart was still beating fast. He stopped and took a deep breath. He heard jeering laughter and looked up at the terrace on the third floor. The young girl laughed again.

"Shahrazad," a woman standing behind her said, "aren't you ashamed?"

He gave the two young men a strange look. They leered at him and laughed.

The thin one stopped. "What's the matter with you?" he asked Shahrayar. "Aren't you happy?"

"Shahrayar, come on, leave him alone," the fat one said to the thin one. "Can't you see how he is?"

Shahrayar looked at the two of them and walked away.

He began to make a great effort to avoid looking at people. If only my obsessions were about objects instead of people, he thought. I could stare at them until I went insane or this odd sensation went away.

He stopped in front of a store display and stared at a picture of a beautiful Japanese girl. The picture winked at him every time he moved. He went into the store and bought the winking picture. He kept on shifting it in his hand, looking at her winking right eye. He put it in his pocket and crossed to the other sidewalk. He stood in the middle of the walkway by the Wall of the Lazy, smoking and contemplating the sea that he loved so much. A slim girl passing behind him hijacked his gaze away from the scene he was enjoying. He followed her to get back his sea view, now obscured by her turquoise clothes, which blended into the horizon. She stopped and exchanged kisses on both cheeks with another, curvier girl.

"Shahrazad, where have you been all this time?" the thieving girl asked.

Shahrayar stopped opposite them, watching the way they spoke and moved.

"You'd better move along," the eyes of the girl who had stolen his sea view told him. "You'd better move along, before they smash your face."

"What about my sea view?"

"You fool. Don't you see that it turned into the color of my clothes? Strip me of my clothes if you dare. Strip me!"

He could not strip her. I've seen that robber girl before somewhere, he told himself as he entered Café Paris. I've seen her; I've certainly seen her. I don't remember where. My memory's beginning to fade.

He sat down and ordered coffee with milk. Ah! I remember now. *I saw her in this café. She was sitting over there near the door, with a fat woman reading a magazine full of photos, a thin man, and a curvy girl who was younger than her. The girls were talking about Fez and Tangier, and about obesity and slimness, while the thin man was silently reading his Arabic newspaper. That day I thought she had a Fez accent. She was so happy about the way I was staring at her that the glass of orange juice slipped out of her hand onto the table. Her white clothes got stained, and she headed for the washroom. Before she came back,*

I hurried away. Now, here she is today, taking her gaze back from me, with her beautiful turquoise clothes. She has every right to take it back. That day, I was the one who robbed her.

A slim man and fat woman were sitting relaxed in front of him in the corner by the door. The man was reading his Arabic newspaper and the woman was perusing a magazine written in Latin letters. The fat waiter poured him some coffee.

"Mr. Shahrayar, is that enough?"

Shahrayar gave him a strange look.

"Pour it all."

The waiter poured all the coffee from the little metal pot, then added milk.

"What's wrong? Has something happened to you?"

"Nothing. Everything is normal."

"You don't seem normal this morning."

As usual, Shahrayar paid the waiter for his coffee ahead of time.

"It's just a feeling, Mr. Shahrayar. Just a feeling," Shahrayar told him, as he gave him that strange look.

The fat waiter smiled and left. He put sugar in the cup and took two sips before stirring it. He focused his strange gaze on the fat woman. She became agitated and looked at the thin man who was with her. The man looked at her, then at Shahrayar, whose gaze was focused on the woman. His gaze was as rigid as a statue. The man stood up and came over to Shahrayar.

"What's wrong?"

"Nothing. Everything is normal."

"Why are you staring at my wife like that?"

"Never! I was looking at something else."

"You're lying to me. I saw you looking at her."

"Not at all. I was looking at something behind her."

"What's that thing behind her that you were staring at?"

"It's my business."

"Your business!"

"Yes, I was looking at that tree."

The man turned toward the tree on the sidewalk.

"So, you're mocking me."

"Shahrayar," his wife Shahrazad told him, "come back and forget about him,"

"Dog!" the man said to Shahrayar.

Shahrayar remembered the fat dog dragging the slim girl.

I wish I could run over, he thought, and use this skinny man to hit that dog.

The man went back to his seat. The slim girl who had just taken back her stolen gaze came in, along with her chubby friend.

"Shahrazad, hello!" the fat woman said to the first, slim Shahrazad.

They exchanged loud kisses, then the two Shahrazads sat down.

"Where have you been all this time?" the fat woman said to the first, slim Shahrazad.

"In Fez. I've been very busy. And you, Shahrazad?"

"In Tangier. Where did you think I'd go?"

"Isn't your father Mr. Shahrayar al-Hajjaj?" the man asked the second Shahrazad, the chubby one.

"Yes. He's my father."

"I know your father. I know your mother, Shahrazad, as well. You were still very young when I used to give private lessons to your brother Shahrayar and your sister Shahrazad at your house."

"When we used to live in the Kasbah."

"Exactly. You were a baby learning how to walk."

"I don't remember."

She leaned her elbow on the edge of the table.

"What's your name?"

"Did you forget my name?" she asked, surprised.

"You were very young. You were walking, but you couldn't speak yet."

"My name's Shahrazad."

"How old are you?"

"Sixteen."

"You've grown."

She smiled at him and tilted her head. The fat waiter was standing in front of them. The first and second Shahrazads ordered orange juice.

"Are you all going to spend the whole summer here?" the third, fat Shahrazad asked the first, slim Shahrazad.

"Yes."

"What about your mother?"

"She'll come here with my sister Shahrazad. I'm waiting for them."

The waiter put down a glass and filled it halfway from the first bottle of orange juice. Then he put down a second glass and filled it halfway from the second bottle of orange juice. He then turned around and faced Shahrayar.

"You'd better go home, Mr. Shahrayar," he said, "and get some rest. You don't seem well this morning."

Shahrayar looked at him and shook his head without speaking.

"Did you hear what I just said?" the waiter asked.

Shahrayar shook his head at him and gave him a strange

look. Once the waiter had left, Shahrayar focused his peculiar gaze on the first, slim Shahrazad. As had happened the other day, the glass slipped from her hand onto the table and spilled over her turquoise-colored clothes. They all turned and looked at Shahrayar, whose gaze was focused on the first, slim Shahrazad. His gaze was as rigid as a statue.

The man stood up and confronted Shahrayar.

"Shahrayar, listen!" his wife told him, "come back and forget about him!"

Tangier, 1972

Talking About Flies
Is Banned

I never regretted the days in prison that I did not count. It was the torture I thought about more than the time, though my days did pass with difficulty.

Two hours or more have passed. Now I know for sure that I can lose all sense of time and connectedness to the outer world in less time than I have ever imagined. Several times I wondered why they were delaying the start of my torture session.

The car stops. I feel it slowing down. The door opens. I did not see the man who yelled, "Get out!"

I wondered if this was a trick for the start of my torture. I hesitated.

"Get out, I said!" I heard the call a second time.

I get out, trembling, craning my neck. I'm feeling dizzy and lose my balance. It makes me feel heavy. The cold night breeze slaps me. I am pushed forward. The car rolled backward a bit. I almost fall down. I hear the rear door of the car swinging open, then closing.

The landscape is large and empty, a mix of misery and luxury. Where is this city? No doubt somewhere in the North. Why have they moved me to another city? Do they want to create new problems here? From darkness to darkness. In darkness they arrested me, and in darkness they released me.

A sound from behind. "This night will be your night," a man tells his girlfriend. "Tonight, you'll find out who I am."

"Do whatever you want with me," she replies, "but you're wrong. We only drank; I didn't allow myself to sleep with him."

"Huh! Tell that to some other idiot!"

They walked past me, their voices gradually fading. They swayed, stopped, and stared at each other. He pulled her toward him and pressed himself against her. He tried to push her down.

"Ah, ah, ah . . . !" she groaned in pain. "Please, not here!" she begged.

"You deserve this here. You deserve more than this here."

"People, people are watching. Please, don't do this to me here!"

"I don't care about people. I'm going to do this to you here."

He pushed her down. He undid his belt.

"Please. Do whatever you want to me, but not here."

He got up, swayed, and walked away from her. She got up swaying and followed him. Nothing can be created unless its form has existed previously. That may be true, yet isn't it absurd?

I walk carefully and slowly. Another person approaches me. He stops and faces me, leaning on a garbage can in the street; he talks to it:

"What's the matter with you? You're empty now, aren't you? Who put a hole in you? Who emptied you?"

"You don't want to tell the truth," he went on, "but people know. They put a hole in you and left you here. Talk to me, my dear—my dear tin can. They abandoned you, didn't they?"

He gave me a sorrowful look. He was throttling me in the air, or maybe pretending to throttle someone else. From a distance, I saw him glance at me once again, but then he disappeared.

There was a big picture on the wall at the alley entrance of an artist, as usual, an actor or singer. But no, what's this? It's my picture. Why? What for? It was getting clearer and clearer. I do not know how this picture of me was taken so clearly and precisely without my being aware of it.

Amarouche Telimsani. It is forbidden to have dealings with this person under any circumstances. Anyone who does not abide by this warning and has dealings with him will be punished by law.

So is that the torture? Is that what they've come up with? There are some other pictures in the alleyway with torn edges. One picture on a wall has the eyes ripped out. No doubt the person who vandalized the picture wants them to put out *my* eyes. It's likely they'd do it if they felt like it. They can do even more. Can no one stop them?

Copies of my picture were stuck everywhere: shops, cafés, restaurants, exits and entrances. That was probably the case in other cities as well.

I reached the café square. It was small but still seemed larger than the other big square. My picture was on the storefronts and walls. I saw people pointing at me and staring. I felt a vacuum in my whole body. I took a seat in the Café Central. One waiter was asleep. Another waiter came out from behind the counter and woke him up.

"Please, get out of here!" the waiter said to me, rubbing his eyes.

I stared at him.

"You know very well why," he added.

I thanked him with a nod and left. So it was not that the people held a grudge against me. They were simply obliged not to deal with me. Any attempt to sit down in another café would be absurd, the same rejection. Perhaps some of them would set about humiliating me, and I would not be able to defend myself.

Around the corner, I spotted a small restaurant. In the window display were fried fish, reddened roasted chickens, raw steaks, boiled eggs, and spices. I stopped by the storefront. Men and women were smoking and drinking, empty plates and leftover food on the table in front of them. They were laughing, flirting, and joking. The sleepy waiter got up quickly and slowly approached the door. He did not say anything, but merely stared curiously at me from head to toe. His eyes were saying, "Hey! Scram! Get away from my restaurant's doorway."

I walked away, sounds of laughter echoing behind me. I noticed five or six heads following me with their gaze, though none of them crossed the threshold of the restaurant. Should I keep banging my head against the wall until I fall? That will be a form of torture that I choose for myself. But how can I be sure that it's the best solution for my problem? Won't there be another one?

I left one street and entered the next, on and on. I went up the stairs, exhausted. The terrace was beautiful. From up there, the view of the sea was amazing, water shining under the lights of ships just like a mirage. I sat down on a granite bench.

How am I going to face my destiny? Is this the only kind of torture? How long will it last? I stretched out on the bench, my exhaustion gradually easing. This court ruling may be a mere farce, with me as its hero and its audience the residents of this city. Perhaps my case will be the beginning of a new legal application. Anything is possible as long as there are people who want to entertain themselves at the expense of others. The ruling may also be simultaneous punishment and entertainment. Anything's possible.

I fell asleep. I felt a hand take my wallet out from my back pocket. I woke up from a vibrant dream.

"Stay still," a man said. "We aren't going to hurt you."

"You know very well that from now on, you won't need any more money," a second man added. "You won't even need yourself."

I said nothing.

"You can go back to sleep if you want," the first man said. "I don't think anyone will hurt you."

They moved away, looking elegant as they descended the stairs, laughing. They disappeared as if they were going down into a well. So they know everything about my case and my fate. They know more about me than I know myself. Is all this happening just because I wrote an article about begging? I had forgotten all about my wallet. Strange. Why hadn't the people who put me in prison taken it, or those who released me? I think my case must be more serious than I imagine.

Voices were approaching. Two, three, five . . . All at once, they started stripping me of my clothes. One of them kept coughing in my face. I was scared, but I calmed down when none of them got rough with me. Weird. Even these homeless men are treating me with kindness—well behaved and happy.

One after the other they left, each of them examining what he had stolen. They left me completely naked. No doubt they, too, knew everything about me. They knew that I would not need to cover my nakedness. I don't blame them since actually I would not even be needing myself. Fair enough, they needed things that I didn't.

I started shivering. So then, my case was not a farce meant to entertain people. Three people: the first carrying a bucket, the second a white cloth, and the third a small red box. They sat down on the bench to my left, staring blankly into the void. They smoked. I shifted my position. They looked at me with worried expressions.

"Listen," one of them said, "if you like, we can start on you before sunrise."

"It's going to be hot today," the second one added. "Just like every day now. I think it's going to get even hotter."

"No one will be able to sympathize with you," the third continued. "They might be sympathetic from afar, but under these circumstances no one can help you."

"One day, two days, three, then you will collapse. I don't think you can stand much more. Imagine yourself sitting here naked, or moving from one place to another. No one will hurt you, but people are going to regard you as a strange, caged animal. Wouldn't it be better for us to start carrying out your sentence now? If we start now, it will lessen your suffering, and you'll be saving us time on this tedious task."

"I still don't understand why they issued such a verdict," I said, addressing the one who had spoken first.

"Because you mocked people more than you should have," he replied.

I was shocked. "I don't think I mocked people," I told him. "I wrote about a prevalent phenomenon."

"That's how you see it. It was unprecedented, the way you mocked people."

"That's right," one of the other men said. "You went too far mocking people."

"And you had no right to ignore the law," the other two noted, "especially the new law."

"Yes. Ignorance of the law doesn't exempt you from punishment. That's the statute, and even though it's old, it's still in operation."

"You're lucky. It seems they went easy on you."

"Despite all that," I said, "I don't deserve such punishment."

"How is it that you don't deserve such punishment when you know that the flies died about twenty-five years ago?"

"The flies?" I replied, astonished.

"Yes, the flies have been extinct for a quarter of a century, and yet you're writing today about their sexual activity."

"But I didn't write about the sexual activity of flies," I replied angrily. "I wrote an article about begging."

"If only you had. It's possible they wouldn't have convicted you, if you'd at least written about something real. But when you write about something that doesn't exist, it's a major crime."

"I assure you, I wrote nothing about flies."

"Listen, don't try to get smart with us. We don't care whether you wrote about flies, or beggars, or women peeing in the streets. We're only trying to make you understand that you have a serious problem."

"In my case, though," I said, "there must be a mistake."

"It's because of your bad luck. The sentence has been passed."

"In that case," I said after a moment, "you must execute the punishment."

"No, not us. We're only tasked with guarding you and making sure you don't suffer. We'll hand you over to people whose job it is to carry out the punishment."

"Where?"

"Come with us."

They got up. They were all carrying things, and I walked in front of them.

"Oh, you forgot the soap," one of them said.

I figured they meant camphor soap. They carried all the tools of death. It was strange that they were keen to observe custom in the burial of a deceased person accused of some kind of wrongdoing. We passed through the small square. This time, it looked dirty and sad. We were followed by people who were emerging from big holes, like rats. Two workers paused, cleaning dirty drains. The stench was dreadful, but I did not hold my breath the way I would have in the past. What did it matter now whether the smell was good or bad?

When we reached the large square, another line of rats emerged. They were chatting, screaming, and laughing. I slipped on a fruit peel and fell backward. There were loud sneering laughs. Two of my escorts helped me up.

"Are you all right?" one of them asked me.

"Not too bad," I replied. "Still walking."

Monkeys—they were still eating fruit like monkeys. They were defecating in the streets like dogs. And despite all that, they claimed flies were extinct.

I walked in front of them, limping. My left leg was hurting, but nothing mattered anymore. I heard words such as *burial, victim, punishment, new law* . . .

For around half an hour we walked within a green darkness. Only four or five people were left who continued to follow the caravan, walking behind us.

By the time we reached the white field, even they had disappeared.

"We've arrived," the pallbearer told me.

The door of the eternal silence was open. When I entered, a night breeze slapped me, perfumed and cold. The door of a small house opened, and two strongmen appeared, giants in black clothes.

Tangier, 1972

Bashir, Dead or Alive

He took out a handful of ground tobacco and began to roll it in a piece of a lottery ticket.

"Why a lottery ticket?" Badri asked.

"That's the way he's been doing it since he lost his fortune," Baba Jilali replied. "For him, a losing lottery ticket is like an English pound or a dollar, a hundred pesetas or a thousand francs. In his youth, he sold a piece of land, part of his inheritance, to the British Consulate. Part of the land that he sold was a private cemetery. People accused him of heresy: 'You sold the land of your forefathers!' That is how they tormented him.

"'I sold them the dead,' is how Bashir responded, 'but you're selling the living.'

"He obtained British protection. He booked a room in the Cecil Hotel so he could get to know visiting foreigners. He bought a horse and a pistol. He was granted a gun permit, something usually given only to foreign nationals. He started threatening that he would shoot his antagonists, but he would give money to people who knew how to treat him well. People started feeling intimidated by his new status. They would swallow his insults and put up with his strange behavior without objection. At night, he would go to Cabaret Imperial, a brothel, which today has turned into a clothing store.

"Señora Rosita would welcome him with fear and respect.

"'Señor Bashir!' she would say, 'try to treat her gently tonight! She's a nice girl, and lonely in this town. She's the best girl I have, you know. It's just circumstances that have forced her to live this hard kind of life.'

"For just a moment, Bashir would chuckle scornfully. Then he'd demand loudly, 'Where is she? Where's your little Sevillian girl?'

"Susana would arrive, whimpering, shy, scared. He would pull her to him and embrace her savagely. None of the other patrons could protest in his presence.

"'He's crazy!' they all thought. 'Crazy and savage!'

"He would take her to the love room and order the most expensive wine.

"'Señora Rosita, isn't there something of higher quality than this?'

"'No, Señor Bashir. This's the finest wine we have.'

"He rarely finished with Susana without making her burst into tears. Yet she grew accustomed to his savageness and perverse sexual behavior. She stopped complaining to the brothel owner.

"Even the children in the Petit Socco knew who Bashir was. It was to that square that he would go in daytime. He would hand the reins of his horse to any of the people who raced to offer him assistance, then he'd go to Café Raqassa to greet the friends of his father and legendary forebears in Tangier.

"'Does anyone have any complaints?'

"'No, we're all fine, thanks be to God,' one of them would

volunteer to answer. 'May God extend his blessing to us and you.'

"He would smoke a little hashish with them and boast about his grandfathers, who were buried in Tangier. He would join in in cursing newcomers to the city. Then he would go back to the center of the Petit Socco and strut happily for a time in the middle of the square before entering Café Central.

"'This city no longer has a customs office,' he would yell. 'It's turned into a donkeys' stable. Every single day, our city's being marred by faces we don't recognize; we've no idea where they come from.'

"Then, for a moment, he would gaze at the new faces.

"He would sit by himself, not allowing anybody to sit with him. He would take out one British pound, a dollar, one hundred pesetas, or a thousand francs, put the money on the table, and wait until the new eyes noticed it. Taking out the bag of tobacco, he would roll a cigarette using the banknote, his manner full of pride and arrogance. Their eyes would pop out—all the eyes, both old and new.

"Sometimes one of them would walk by him and say, 'Long live Bashir!'

"Bashir would guffaw like a Roman emperor at play. He might order the waiter to offer the man a drink as he blew smoke from his thick cigar. If a beggar approached him, he would take a coin and look at it, flip it in the air, and catch it before giving it to the beggar.

"In the evening, he would ride his horse along the empty seashore. He used to perform crazy equestrian feats. Once he drank so much that he fell off his horse. No one dared approach him, and he stayed there the entire night, suffering from his bruises, with the horse neighing beside him. Before sunset, he would often take off his clothes and swim far out, while his horse waited on the shore.

"Those people with eyes on the sea and ears on the ground said, 'Mohamed saw him—and he's a pious man as you know—kissing his mistress, the mermaid that comes to him every evening from the depths of the sea. His father, too—May God rest his soul in peace—was married to a mermaid.'

"That was what the people familiar with the city in its glory days knew about him. He had been well off until just before the Spanish Civil War, but then one night they saw him sleeping on the doorstep of the Grand Paris store. Those who knew him realized that Bashir had gone bankrupt."

A small commotion erupted near Bashir, and Baba Jilali stopped talking. They saw a bold young man using his body to shade Bashir from the sun. Bashir was kneeling on the ground, muttering and waving with his hands, but the young man was persistent.

"Ah! You seller of the dead! You eater of cemetery greens! You abuser of young and old! You cat protector and human hater! You eater of dead chickens!" He laughed, then repeated his words in a loud voice.

Badri moved to intervene, but Baba Jilali caught his arm. "Stay where you are! Don't get involved in what doesn't concern you."

"But it's an insult!"

With a crazy lunge, Bashir grabbed the young man's legs. He fell over with a scream. Bashir wildly bit into his hairy calf. A circle of spectators formed and, with a little effort, managed to release the young man from Bashir's hands.

"Did he hurt you?"

The young man did not respond. Shame clouded his face.

"He scared you, didn't he?"

Bashir laughed hysterically. His face was like an old Chinese man's, his mouth like a gaping vagina, his eyes wrinkled and dark. The commotion around Bashir calmed down. Tears of victory burst from his small round eyes, eyes like those of an owl. He laughed like a fish gasping for breath.

"And then what happened, Baba Jilali?" Badri asked.

"He got used to going to the cemetery every day. During the night, he used to collect greens and cook them along with his food at the beach, all of which reminded him of the days when he was wealthy. When he ate the greens that sprouted from the cemetery dead, he believed that he was taking revenge on humanity, both dead and alive.

"'I'll wait for you there in the cemetery,' he told one of his tormenters. 'I'll eat your greens raw.'"

Baba Jilali paused for a moment.

"That's Bashir," he went on. "He's lost the meaning of time and place, from the cemetery to the shore and from the shore to the Petit Socco."

Badri ran with the people hurrying to the cemetery, "Call the police," he heard one of them urging. "Don't let him get away. He's going to come back to dig up the graves."

Badri asked a young man what was going on.

"An old man named Bashir wants to make the cemetery a burial place for dead animals," he responded.

"Is this the first time Bashir has wanted to bury one of his cats there?" another person inquired.

"Who knows? Maybe he's buried other animals before—but today he wants to bury a dead cat."

Badri saw Bashir sitting on a tomb. The dead cat was at his feet, the hole unfinished, and next to it was a stick that he seemed to have been using to dig. Bashir was silent. He looked defiantly at the crowd and calmly at the small, spotted dead cat. After a moment, he got up and turned his back on the crowd. Taking his penis out, he pissed on a tomb.

"Hey! What're you doing, Bashir?"

People muttered among themselves, and then there was silence.

"Should we stop him?"

"No. Let him do as he pleases. At least we'll be witnesses to what he's doing."

"He's crazy. No one can blame someone who's crazy."

"May God protect us from humans like this!"

"God creates whatever he wants."

"May God grant us a good end."

"Yes! God, please let our end be better than our beginning."

"May God protect us from the evil he created."

"And the guard! Where is he?"

"This cemetery doesn't have a guard anymore."

"Oh, he's probably buried many other cats here."

"Maybe. I've heard things about him. I didn't believe it until I'd seen for myself what I'm seeing now."

"People from his generation say that he inherited the cemetery land from his ancestors and then sold it."

Bashir shook the piss off his penis. He sat on the edge of the tiled tomb, buttoning his pants.

"I'm surprised he's so calm. He's acting as if he's done nothing shameful."

"Don't you see that he's crazy? Who's more liberated than a crazy man who does whatever he wants?"

"It's strange, the serenity of people who are crazy."

Bashir took a wrinkled lottery ticket from his pocket. He started rolling a thick cigarette.

"He might as well take a dump in front of us, for all the good our surrounding him is doing."

He lit his cigarette.

"But look, he doesn't see us. Now he's smoking. What's the difference between a man or an animal dying? That's what he wants us to understand."

"He's right. What's the big deal if a cat is buried next to a human?"

"Nothing. Our people simply aren't accustomed to it."

"God creates what he wants."

"So Bashir is making us accustomed to it."

"May God protect us from the evil he created."

A few drops of rain fell. Some people began to withdraw.

"Come on, let's go!" one of them said. "What do we have to do with a man who wants to bury a cat next to a human? To everyone his destiny."

"You're right. Everyone buries his mother the way he wants."

"Whoever cuts a branch should drag it himself. The man must finish alone what he starts."

As the people hurried away, heavy rain started falling. Bashir remained like a statue on the tomb. Badri moved under the willow tree to watch Bashir finish burying the cat. The cemetery was soon empty of people. A small mound formed over the place where he had buried the cat. He smoothed it with his hands as the rain poured down. And yet Bashir seemed to have power over everything.

A sunny day. People come alive on the streets as if they have been asleep the whole winter. Flocks of sparrows in the sky prove to them the brightness of that blessed day. Bats outside the cave groom themselves. Chatting merrily, the people point to the sun: the mythology of memory yawns in their minds. They speak of that day as if they had never lived one like it before. They stare at women's faces, their bosoms, their bottoms, especially the rounder ones, and then fix their gaze on underwear and garters beneath their transparent skirts. The women snatch glances, often shyly, but it is strange that in their gossip they remark on a missing button, a piece of white thread noticed on a black vest.

"You men cannot even go out in the street," one of the women comments, "without something about you catching our eye."

They walk fast, stop abruptly, then resume walking as if they had forgotten something and were worried that it was about to explode or get stolen. It was as if they had diarrhea. They were ready to rant in the face of whoever would spoil such a bright, springlike day.

Badri found himself walking aimlessly in the Grand Socco. He had no woman and no children, yet he wanted to find himself alongside a sedate woman and quiet children. A strong, attractive woman passed in front of him.

"Oh, the fur of the goat! I hear those furry women are horny. But I do not like women who have goat legs. I have enough fur myself. Is it not enough that their hidden hair is as thick as a cushion? I want her smooth as a snake or a fish. That's how I want her."

Someone bumped into him from behind: "Sorry, I'm . . . "

Badri shook his head. Now other people began crashing into each other. Badri watched them coming toward the boulevard of the Tree Hotel. The handle of a basket slipped from the hand of a pregnant Spanish woman. "I like pregnant women. Their appearance inspires respect." Half the basket's contents tumbled out: tomatoes, potatoes, eggs, asparagus, beets, oysters, and apples.

"Hey, you! Are you blind?" the woman shouted in the face of a young man in a hurry. "Everybody catches the infection from a crazy person."

The young man did not turn back toward her. Badri saw her bend over with difficulty to pick up a tomato that had stopped rolling.

Potatoes beat tomatoes, he thought, laughing to himself, because they don't spoil.

Badri hurried along with the others. The event at their destination had to be important. He saw a crowd there: people pushing each other; mutterings, questions, movement; young men rubbing against the bottoms of young women. Badri saw a body half covered with a piece of burlap, and next to it a dead chicken without a trace of blood at its neck.

"Who died?" he asked.

"An elderly man named Bashir. They saw him stumble and fall."

He finally died his own death. Not for anyone else's sake. Perhaps that is what they'll say about him. They only feel any sorrow for people who die for their sake. What annoys me, Badri thought, is that one has no choice but to deal with others, like it or not.

"How happy he is! He died without suffering."

"He lived alone. He must have suffered."

"And that dead chicken?"

"He probably caught it to eat. They say that he cooked dead animals with the greens of the dead."

"Poor man!"

"He buries what he doesn't eat, and he eats whatever is edible, dead or alive."

"Does he have any family?"

"Perhaps, but what matters to the family now? Everything ends here. From the moment that he fell, he belonged to no one, not even to himself."

"He must've died of cardiac arrest."

"The autopsy will reveal that."

"Perhaps the bad food he ate poisoned him."

"Even that doesn't matter now. He's dead. 'If it's time for the end, they shall not live one hour more or one hour less.'"

"Yes. Wherever you are, death will find you."

"Did he die for real?"

"Yes, he's dead."

"What was the cause of death?"

"No one knows. He died, period."

"He died like some animal that he buried in the cemetery. Like that chicken that he hadn't eaten yet."

"But why are we talking about him like this?"

"True, we'll all die. We must respect death."

Two police officers appeared, clearing the way. One of them made it his job to move the crowd away while the other one approached the corpse. He bent over the lump, lifted the burlap covering the head, and assessed it for a moment. Then he folded back the cloth and took Bashir's wrist in his hand.

"He's alive," he shouted. "He's still alive."

"He's still alive!"

The corpse moved.

"He isn't dead yet."

"Alive!"

"Alive?"

"Alive?"

"Yes, he's alive. Not dead. They took him for dead."

"Strange!"

"Yes, he's still alive. He'll live again after being dead."

"He's lucky."

"Move back. The man is still alive. Are you listening? He's alive, not dead!"

"Strange! He's alive."

The officer moved the piece of burlap aside. The other officer approached his colleague. The ring of people huddled around the two officers.

"He must've just fainted," someone said.

"They took him for dead though he was alive."

"Back up, people. The man's still alive. He's alive, not dead. Do you hear?"

"They don't believe it."

"Back up! Disperse!"

"They didn't feel for the pulse correctly."

Astonishment and confusion. While some people in the crowd awaited resurrection, others prepared to run away. Sheer horror doubled the astonishment on their faces.

"Bring water. What are you waiting for?"

"The key! The key!" an old lady shouted. "Put the key in his hand."

"Yes! Give him a key and some water."

"But no, he didn't fall because of a seizure."

"Then putting a key in his hand won't harm him. It's only a key. Put a key in his hand! A key in the hand can't hurt."

Lifting him by his arms and thighs, the two officers carried Bashir over to a wall and leaned him up against it. People backed away in fear. Mutterings, questions, pushing from forward and behind. His eyelids were closed, his mouth taut; his hands drooped.

"Here's the water."

The officer brought the cup close to the wrinkled, slack mouth. Bashir cringed a little, then drank. He opened his eyes and moved his arms.

"If they'd put a piece of glass over his mouth and nose to check his breathing, they would not have made this mistake."

"He will continue to scare people if he stays alive."

"And if he dies, as the prophets have died before him?"

"They'll look at him as if he were a ghost walking among them."

"But he did live like a ghost among people."

From now on, Badri thought, the man's mere passing in front of them will make people think of death walking in a living body. How is it possible for a man to live if he dies in people's imagination? What a legend, one that can erase the truth! What is the truth? Is it that a human being can die while not yet dead?

The ambulance arrived. Two men got out.

"They're going to take you for treatment," the officer informed Bashir.

Bashir gave them both a resigned look. He let the paramedics lift him.

There was a commotion in the crowd.

"A dead person is resurrected! This is so strange!"

"People are stupid. The man only fainted, and still they insist that he's rising from the dead!"

"Look! His chicken's still there! What if his chicken also rises? What do you think will happen?"

"They'll all faint. They'll run away like mice. They'll go crazy."

One of the officers kicked the chicken aside, while the other officer got into the ambulance with Bashir.

"So now," the officer who stayed behind shouted, "are you waiting for someone else to faint?"

They looked at each other, smiling. Mutterings, stirrings. As the ambulance left, they began to move. Many of them seemed not to believe what had just happened.

Tangier, 1967

Vomit

The stench of death is everywhere. People look at one another strangely, without using words. No one walks with anyone else. The trees are stripped bare. The light breeze scoops up the dry leaves, which alight on the doorsteps of houses and on public benches. The walkers search for places where there is a scent of life. They vomit. They chase away the flies. They walk indifferently over the vomit, pus, and corpses. They avoid bodies on the brink of death. Some of them fall into their vomit and do not get back up. Shops, cafés, and restaurants are all closed.

A man is panting. He wheels around and looks back. He totters, then falls. Fighting exhaustion, he falls. His piece of bread slips out of his hand. He crawls and grasps it. He takes a bite eagerly. A second person appears, his face bleeding. Silently they face each other. Angrily they move apart. Agitated, they lunge at each other and clash, but without much force. The piece of black bread slips from the first one's hand. Their hands hang limp. They totter, bleeding heavily. They face each other, then move apart. Gathering their strength and scowling, they become agitated again. Drawing closer, they try to grab each other. Their hands are paralyzed, and they bump against each other. They groan and bleed. The first one groans and falls down. Then the second totters. Trying to grab at thin air, he falls on top of the first one.

Arsalane leaves his seat on the public bench calmly—but he is exhausted. His foot slips, and he falls on his hands and knees. Through the fog of his eyes the piece of black bread looks small. A blonde girl is approaching, exhaustedly dragging herself. He crawls quickly, rests, then crawls quickly again. He has one eye on the piece of black bread and the other on the blonde girl. He crawls and crawls, quickly. His hands slip on a small pool of blood and vomit. Standing up, he wipes his hands on his pants and shakes his numb leg in the air. Tottering, he limps and extends his leg into the void. With every step, the piece of bread grows in his eyes. They move toward the piece of bread, which now is shrinking in his eyes. Sometimes it grows, but then it starts shrinking.

They stand facing each other, staring. Her eyes are big, deep, sad, and tired. He contemplates the dead puppy in her arms. The puppy's eyes are protruding, tearful, screaming. He moves, yet his whole face is bleeding heavily. Desperately he extends his trembling hands toward the piece of bread. He crawls little by little, his slender, veined hands reaching forward. The bread is shrinking more in Arsalane's eyes. He bends over quickly, and the blood throbs painfully in his head. The red fog thickens. He staggers and steadies himself. He is afraid of falling and not being able to get up again. There are fresh bloodstains on the piece of bread. He tears it and puts a piece in her hand. The beggar groans. Arsalane puts half of the piece in his hand, and the beggar clutches it nervously. Arsalane moves on, as does the girl. They eat voraciously. They move away from each other. He goes back to the bench. Turning his back on the city, he contemplates the sunrise, the sea, and the garden flowers. A child snatches a sandwich from the corpse's hand. Someone is vomiting down below, and someone else up above. A dog laps up the yellow vomit. The person stops vomiting. The dog is waiting for more. The person falls onto his face, his mouth gaping open. The dog runs away, frightened. The pale girl sobs. The two men start to fight, biting each other. One takes out a knife, but the other one grabs it and tries to stab the former. The former pokes the latter in the eye with his finger and retrieves his knife. The latter screams like an animal and presses his palms to his eyes. He falls down, vomiting blood and wallowing in it. His throat rattles. The former now grabs the girl by her long blonde hair. She groans as he kisses her fiercely. She collapses limp onto his chest, in a faint. Her lips are bleeding. He tries to lift her, then drags her by her hands. He pauses. His mouth is bleeding too. He drags her, then pauses. One of her shoes slips off as he drags her, then the second shoe slips off as well. Her bottom half is stripped naked as he keeps dragging her. Her dress is ripped, and her feet and legs are bleeding. He falls backward, then gets back up. He falls again and gets back up again. He takes her toward the fenced garden.

Arsalane observes them thoughtfully. The girl is still, unconscious, and the man is still, panting. In Arsalane's mind desire is blending with the sunrise and the sea, with flowers and birds of the morning, with the buzzing of flies and the dry black bread. In his senses that desire blends with the stench of vomit and death, and a long silence.

Tangier, 1971

Bald Trees

Huge. Its beak curved, its claws long and sharp. Bald. Burning sun. The trees of this region had not grown leaves in a long time. The shadows of their branches were blunt, thin. On some only the trunk remained. Most were burned, and fire and termites had whittled away many of these. Emaciated human corpses, military fatigues, shoes, helmets; destroyed military equipment, some of it still intact. Everything scattered across the vast landscape was either destroyed or burned. The sun was like a hot iron. There was no sign of human life. Vultures circled here and there or crouched on the dry trees or around the corpses.

Huge. Its beak curved, its claws long and sharp. Bald. Burning sun. It moved. I moved. It flew and circled above me. Its shadow approached me. Screaming, I called for help and struck at it with my hand. It went to crouch on a severed tree branch. I panted. Damn it! It was not panting like me. It was making fun of me and wearing me out with its ferocious gaze; it was putting me to sleep. Striking out at it consumed my strength. It had forced me into this situation. I was like a turtle flipped on its back under this grueling sun. No doubt it was going to gouge my eyes out, then tear at my innards.

I could see a mirage of waves. My throat was dry as wood.

I tried with all my might to swallow. I felt as if the lining of my throat was being torn apart when I tried to swallow my spittle. I took a pencil out of my shirt pocket and bit it, gnawing at it with great effort. Every time I chewed, a hot liquid filled my mouth.

I gave it a stern look so as not to appear weak. The muscles of my face trembled. My face must have exposed my vulnerability and fear. Damn it! What should I do with this thing? When it moved, I moved just like it. Its massive wings opened; its claws shot out and retracted. It darted toward me. I spat out the bloody splinters that I had not yet fully chewed. It struck with its strong claws, and I hit back with my weak arms, screaming like a madman. It went back to its branch. Beads of sweat were streaming down my forehead, then settling on my burning eyelashes. This time, I looked at it with my left eye. My hands and legs were bleeding. It was sharpening its beak against its claws and protrusions on the tree trunk. In the next round, perhaps it would close my other eye and crouch on me the way it crouched on that branch.

It moved. I screamed. It repositioned itself on the branch. I stared at it insanely. It was mocking me. It moved, but I did not. This time it caught me by surprise, covering me with its beating shadow as I screamed weakly. Its wings were like a gigantic fan, blowing at me. I could not protect my eye with my hand. After a moment of calm, I flipped over onto my back with my eyes covered. I did my best to wipe away the blood that was flowing down my face. I closed my hand over a mosquito that was hovering above my sweaty eyelid. I opened my eye to look up at the tree. It was no longer there. The shreds of a dark-colored shirt fluttered on a branch.

I was no longer capable of swallowing. My head was boiling. I tried to rest, lying facedown on the ground. Choking, I resumed my previous position. Normally, I would feel most relaxed lying facedown, but it no longer felt relaxing. The ground retained the daytime heat all night long. I could feel my heartbeat slowing: *thud . . . thud . . . thud . . . thud . . . thud . . .*

Will I dry out here the way vegetables do in summertime? I tried my voice: "Ah! Ah!" Weak and unfamiliar. After so much groaning, a slight improvement coursed through my body. Even so, I probably won't be able to fight much longer.

Tangier, 1977

The Negative Force

Footsteps approaching. I opened my eyes and grabbed my rifle, which was leaning against the tree. We started fighting with the two rifles' bayonets. He avoided my strike but managed to stab my lower abdomen. I fired my rifle. I grabbed the bayonet, which was stuck deep in my innards. Nothing else was in my hand. I felt myself being pulled forcefully backward. The rope that was pulling me by the shoulders dangled from the tree. Because he was pulling from far away, I could not see where he was. Maybe he was pulling from behind a tree close to this tree, into which I was being drawn. I looked up into its branches. Slowly, slowly, I was being pulled upward. I tried to untie the knot behind my back. They had tied me up while I was asleep. He stopped pulling the rope. My body was hanging about four or five cubits up in the air. Every time I moved, I swung in a circle. As far as I could see, other people were hanging from trees. I swung myself and looked around me. Bodies were hanging by their necks; others were crucified by their hands or feet; and still others were in my position. So I was not the only one.

At night, it felt as though my mouth was filled with glue. The silence in the area was absolute, and the smell was awful. The sky was beautiful: I had never contemplated it before the way I did on that moonlit night, perhaps because I could not see anything other than the sky. So many things only seem that wonderful when I'm exhausted or sick! But my situation now was much worse than any fatigue or illness.

"What are you doing?"

"I'm shooting at the sky's ugliness."

"But what's in the sky is immortally beautiful."

"What's in the sky dies too. The beautiful and ugly both die. Death occurs both on earth and in the sky."

"Kill what's on the earth first, before trying to kill what's in the sky. If you manage to kill what's on earth, it'll be easier for you to kill what's in the sky."

"No, no. If you kill what's in the sky, half of what's on the earth will die as a result. Maybe even everything on earth will die."

I slept and had a dream. I wet my pants. The smell of my urine surrounds me. Once more, I contemplate the sky as I've never done before. I contemplate it the way I contemplate the sky of my soul during days of illness and despair. The shapes of clouds in the moonlight look like animals that have entered the time of negative force. In my imagination, there's a woman lying on a rock; the sun has stripped her bare, and Pacific waves are showering her. Ifrane spring, the beaches of Fiji, Tahiti, Hawaii, Sri Lanka, and all the festivities of the tattooed Atlas.

Tangier, 1977

Puppies' Tails

The little puppy was biting his tail fiercely.

"Saturn, stop, my baby," the owner shouted. "You're going to eat yourself up."

Every time she tried to get close, the puppy threatened her with a rabid snarl. He kept spinning in circles, attacking his tail. His leash spun with him, wrapping itself around his body. She could not stop him. He had already bitten off almost half his tail, but he did not stop. She was crying. He was not yet done with his tail.

A big dog approached. Stray, wild—half donkey, half dog. It pinned the little puppy down, which surrendered to him with pleasure.

"The dog's going to kill him!" the puppy's owner wailed. "Either that or rape him and rip him apart. It's going to suffocate my little baby!"

Both dogs snarled whenever she tried to get close. They had fun together. An elderly man who was familiar with dogs and their idiosyncrasies came by.

"Ma'am," he told her, "don't worry about your puppy. Fate is being merciful to you, because it's sent you this dog to salvage the situation . . . It's a doctor," he added. "If only you believe, it's going to heal your puppy's dangerous wound. Its

magical ointment will heal him. Maybe it will also immu-
nize him against other diseases that you can't see."

When the elderly man said that, the sad woman stopped
wailing.

"Your puppy has reached puberty, so don't worry about
anything."

The dogs panted together, as the man and owner watched.
The animals were like an old couple. Their rosy tongues dangled and pulled back as they licked each other. They kept ad-
justing their positions relative to each other. They panted excitedly. Then they calmed down without causing any pain or
drawing blood. When the lady realized that the man's pre-
diction was correct, her mind was put at ease. Her face lit
up as she noticed the shadow of goodness in the face of the
old, wise, and respectable man, who seemed to know about
the lives of dogs.

"Take him home and keep him covered as much as you
can," he suggested to her. "For the next two to three days, or
more if possible, feed him well, but not too much. Take him
and keep him covered."

He applied the best and strongest ointments to the
puppy's tail.

"Believe me," he told her again when he saw how happy
she was, "I predict he'll have a better and prettier tail than
before, even."

The wise man, who knew dogs' secrets, told the woman
that. She was reassured by his wise words. With that, the
man disappeared. Before she proceeded home, prayerfully
grateful, she noticed another woman approaching. This
woman too was crying because the same curse had hit her;

the woman was holding a puppy like hers, which was bleeding heavily at his rear.

"What's happened?" the owner asked sympathetically.

"A wandering madman cut off his tail with a knife," the woman replied, "and ran away with it. If I hadn't got to him in time, he would've cut off his ears as well!"

"Why did he do that?"

"He's a wandering madman. He cuts off puppies' tails. If he can, he'll cut off their ears as well."

"But why does he do that to these poor creatures?"

"You wouldn't believe it," the woman said. "He makes soup with them, or cooks them with whatever vegetables, grains, and leftovers he finds."

I will stop here, in this land, wasted because of human disasters. If they had not saved me, I would be nothing more than a bunch of grass. My helmet was thrown under me on the ground, next to my rifle. My eyes were clouding over, and my head was filling up with night fog—red. I felt as though something was tearing at my throat whenever I forced myself to swallow. I could feel similar gashes in my gut.

Tangier, 1977

The Shaved Head

When he awoke in the morning, he washed and carefully inspected his thick hair several times in the mirror . . . He liked his hair; he would be sorry to see it go. He realized that he would not be able to comb it again for two years.

He got dressed and left his apartment. On the third floor, the big dog barked at him from behind the closed door. On the first floor, the little puppy barked at him. By the front door of the building, he saw a man eating the waste from the trash can. His face was burned, his clothes were torn, and he was barefoot. On the opposite sidewalk a miserable dog was licking its lips as it watched the man and trash can. Eating trash made the girls at the clothing factory feel sick. One of them was throwing up curdled milk, and a restaurant waiter was pouring water on the vomit, cursing the morning's disasters. Another girl was wailing, while other girls looked on from a distance, struggling with their disgust. They all felt sorry for the trash eater and prayed to God to have mercy upon his followers who were poor and mad.

The man finished eating from the trash can. He licked his

fingers and wiped his hands on his butt, then moved away a few steps and started peeing on the wall of a building.

He had breakfast in Atlas Café, then he went to the barbershop. He sat in the revolving chair.

"Shave off all my hair," he told the barber.

He was about to travel on the three o'clock train. He had enough time to gather his things together and deliver his apartment key to a friend who would be staying there. He was going to be away from his city for about eighteen months. He might see it on vacation, but it was possible he would never see it again. The barber started wetting his head with warm water. He closed his eyes, recalling the nightmares that had consumed him the night before.

Tangier, 1977

The Poets

The audience awaited the arrival of the procession of poets. There was a platform on the sidewalk of the big street, and books on a table listing the numbers of poets, and a trash can. The audience was silent, all crowded together. Some people moved to the front and craned their necks, looking down the length of the street. More people kept crowding into the street. Their bodies merged as they clung to the edge of the sidewalk. They whispered. The procession of poets appeared, surrounded by guards.

Six poets.

Seven.

No, eight. Nine. There were nine poets.

The eyes of the audience met the poets' gaze, and the poets gazed back.

"Look, their beards are long, and their hair's thick and fluffy."

No doubt they were kept imprisoned in a place where the sun could barely be seen and there was scarcely enough air to breathe.

Never before had there been such an audience. Today its silence seemed solemn. The footsteps of the guards and poets were clearly heard. The audience could not believe what they were seeing. Even the children were silent, their mouths agape. A woman put her hand over the mouth of a little girl who was sobbing silently, gently quieting her.

The poets' jackets were black, numbered on front and back, the numbers big and white. Four guards ascended the wooden steps to the platform, followed by the procession of poets and behind them the rest of the guards. The guards forced them to line up facing the audience. After a moment's silence, the chief of the guards called on poet number 1.

"Come forward and toss your books into the trash can."

The poet did not move. The guard called out a second time in a louder voice, and a third time even louder. Poet number 1 stayed fixed in place. The guard looked threateningly at the poet and pointed at the trash can. The guard then moved to the table, snatched two books with black stickers on them, a number 1 written in white, and tossed them contemptuously into the trash can.

The voice of the chief of guards grew increasingly angry as he continued to call out the numbers of the poets. The guard disposing of the books spat on one before he tossed it into the trash can. The audience seethed. Children cried. Shouts of protest were heard. The guard chief whispered in the ear of the book disposer. All the poets refused. Silence anew. The eyes of the poets met the gaze of the audience, who gazed back.

And thus, just as the poets had ascended the platform, they descended again, back to the place they had come from.

Tangier, 1973

The Coffin

Every evening he would sit in his favorite café, a pack of cigarettes on the table. Often he would order a coffee with milk. He would rub his cigarette to remove any tobacco dust before smoking it. He did not have any friends in this city. His few friends might come to visit from his hometown, or he might meet them there on the weekend.

On days when the weather was nice he would sit in the spacious café, watching passersby or simply musing to himself.

His bedroom was painted dark brown, with thick black curtains drawn day and night. The other room was his painting studio. It was painted deep pink, and the curtains were light blue and translucent. When he entered in the evening, he would prepare warm milk or soup with a handful of garlic powder. Most of his kitchenware was made of pottery or wood. His bedroom furniture was old and basic, bought from a secondhand market. His mattress was wool. He would take off his shoes and sit on the bed in the dark. He would smoke, listening to a recording of Asian pop music or European classical.

Come midnight, he would practice his psychological repose: getting into the coffin dressed in shirt and trousers, with bare feet, then closing the coffin lid. Holes had been drilled in the lid and sides of the coffin. "Living dead and not dying alive," he would say of himself. When he had completed the ritual, he would go into his studio to work.

Now a man stopped in front of him. He was shabbily dressed and bearded; his features were tough and gaunt. Focusing his gaze, the man put an arm around him and drew him close, then kissed him forcefully on the mouth. He straightened up.

"For a long time I've been searching for you in my dreams," he said. "We'll never meet again, of that I am sure."

With a profound look he said farewell and joined the other passersby.

For a moment the man sat there, stunned. Some clients sitting on the café terrace laughed, while others stopped and smiled or stared at him.

"Mr. Nadhel, what happened?" the waiter asked.

"I don't know."

"Does he know you?"

"I don't know."

"Strange. Maybe he's crazy. This city's become full of crazy people."

The people seated around him started whispering to each other and looking at Nadhel. The waiter was standing in front of him. He was feeling dizzy, his eyes were growing clouded. When he left the café, his stunned feelings faded as he slowly walked.

He approached me, taking me by surprise.

"Would you come with me?"

"What did you say?"

"If you please, come with me."

Very skinny, sharp features, tidily dressed. He gave me an intense stare.

"I've been searching for you a long time," he said. "I strongly desire that you accompany me. We might never meet again. Come with me. I miss you. I'll share a secret, one that might interest you."

"Are you crazy, or what?"

"I have a great secret for you."

"Look for a girl as crazy as you are, and tell *her* your great secret."

I laughed at him and left him standing there, glancing back once to make sure he wasn't following me.

I stopped a few girls. They laughed at me scornfully. Near the Spanish-Moroccan bank, I saw her standing in a doorway: blonde, sad, pale, nervous, and so skinny—the kind of stature I like. Her dress was not too tight on her body. I hate girls who wear pants. I went up to her. I thought that I should grab her by the arms as forcefully as that strange man had grabbed me and kiss her. But if I did that, she might not come with me. So I said what I said to other women:

"Would you come with me?"

"Where to?"

"To my apartment."

She let me carry her beautiful small bag stuffed with clothes and walked beside me.

When we got to the entrance of my building, she looked up at the six floors before entering. At the elevator door, I gave her her bag.

"Press floor 3. I usually take the stairs."

In my apartment, I stepped in ahead of her and turned on the hallway light. I pointed the way to the dark bedroom. Inside a ray of light leaked in from the hallway. She sat on the low bed and turned on the small blue table lamp.

"I have beer, whiskey, gin."

"Wine, if you have any."

"I'll go down and buy some from the grocery store."

When he left, a large rectangular object caught my attention. I looked at it for a moment, overwhelmed by curiosity. I stood up, went over to it cautiously, and took another look at it before touching it. With a trembling hand I removed the white cloth covering it. My hair stood on end and my body shook. I ran to the door and opened it, feeling as if some force was pulling me from behind. I lost my balance and tried hard not to fall as I jumped down the stairs. The light went off, and my body kept crashing against the walls, though I was keeping my grip on the handrail. The door of a neighboring apartment opened. I froze as a young girl appeared in a ray of light. I nodded my head in greeting, and she nodded back. She turned the hallway light on; my panting decreased. I continued down the stairs, the girl trailing me.

We met at the entrance of the building. He had a package in his hand. The young girl passed by us.

"What happened? You're not going to stay?"

"No . . . thanks . . . I'll be going." My words came out muffled.

He took out a fifty-dirham banknote and put it in my

hand. I looked at him, regaining some composure. I almost changed my mind. Yet I was still shaking with horror. I thanked him and left.

He turned off the bedside lamp and left the hallway light on. He sat, smoked, and drank from the bottle of wine he'd bought for her. He heard the call to evening prayer from far off. He liked that call more at dawn. The dawn call, he always said, made him embrace his loneliness. He looked at her small bag, and at the coffin that sat there, stripped of its white cloth covering. A live woman that I would like to see dead, and a dead woman that I would have loved had she stayed alive. I fall in love with a dreamlike woman, then I rape her dream. A woman is a raped dream. It is more beautiful that way. There are not enough words to express my discontent. You are afraid of the dead, yet it might be you who killed him. You wander the streets of my city, which are licked by stray, frenetic dogs, while I try to restore my life from a shithole.

He returned to his apartment at noon to have a rest. He did not have any work that evening. Behind the door, he found his sister's scarf, which she used to cover her head. She came once or twice a month to clean his apartment and reorganize the furniture, which got scattered all around the room. He found his brother and sister inside. Some wood was burning in the fireplace, and nearby lay broken pieces of the coffin. His brother had used a hammer to shatter it. They both looked at him, astonished. He just gazed at the blazing fire, saddened by the sound of the crackling wood.

The curtains were not drawn. The rays of the spring sun lit a corner of the room.

He wanted to sit—but then he remembered the painting of the coffin. Going angrily into his studio, he found it in its place. He returned and sat down. Lighting a cigarette, he gazed absentmindedly at what was on fire and what had not burned yet.

"What's happened to you?" his brother asked him.

He pointed to the coffin's rubble. "You both see, that's what happened."

"But what does this coffin stand for?"

"A man who loves coffins bought it for me to paint."

"Do you have to have the coffin in front of you in order to paint it?"

"It's a realistic painting."

"But you always say that abstract is more real than realistic."

"Yes."

"So?"

"This painting was requested by someone, and I must draw it as he requested."

"But you never paint realistic things."

"Yes."

"So?"

"So."

"Why did you paint it?"

"For five thousand dirhams."

"I didn't know that."

"You had no right to destroy the coffin."

"True."

"It's not a good omen to have a coffin in your apartment," his sister said.

"Why?"

"Because it brings doom."

"Who told you that?"

She looked at him, confused.

After a moment of silence, he asked her to return her keys to his apartment. She gave them to him, her eyes full of tears. She placed her hands on her forehead, covering her eyes, and began to cry.

I saw her in the same place. We smiled at each other.

"You didn't come back for your bag."

"Sorry for what happened last time. I went to Tétouan."

"It doesn't matter. I know what scared you."

We walked. A compelling force pushed me to know his mysterious secret. I found wine at his place. He took me to the studio to show me his paintings. The people in his drawings were all ghosts and skeletons. Although they were not flesh and blood, they gathered in the squares, shouting and protesting with their hands and gestures. There were fishing boats abandoned on the beach, often broken. The colors of his drawings were a combination of gray, pale yellow, and crimson; torn nets and an agitated sea. When I asked him about a painting of a crucified person with a nail thrust into his forehead, a couple of nails in his feet, surrounded by a group of ghosts gazing at him, he responded simply:

"People woke up one morning and found him crucified."

I contemplated the painting of the coffin.

"That's why you have a coffin in your apartment."

"After I finished painting the coffin, I also discovered that I could practice psychological exercises."

"Psychological exercises?"

If he slept in it for just an hour, he explained, his fatigue would dissipate and his nerves relaxed. He regained his ability to concentrate. The same Spanish carpenter made him another coffin, secretly working inside his apartment to avoid his neighbors' curiosity, just as he had done the first time.

Although he didn't read a lot, when he did start to read a book, he wouldn't stop until he'd finished. We didn't talk a lot. He bought me Arabic and French novels. He treated me with the utmost kindness.

To please him, I started practicing his psychological exercises with him. The first time I lay down inside the coffin, I was scared, but then it became truly therapeutic.

He left me a letter and three hundred dirhams on the table:

Dear Naima, don't blame me, please. I'm leaving this city and traveling far away—like others who have wished to die in this city, yet left it. The curse of this city is bigger than their own curse. How I adored those vagrants who would jostle every newcomer! They liked their news. They condoned their old and new crimes and their griefs, just as wise men will condone the homeless peeing in the streets.

I don't usually say good-bye to people I love. I don't think we'll meet again. I think that I'll never return. It's best if you go back to Nador. You might have problems, since you don't have proper legal papers or a job anymore. If you need it, take whatever furniture you want. Leave the keys with the doorman. I'll send a letter to my brother to go and pick up the key. I hope you get what you want. With love.

When I finished reading the letter, I felt lonely and scared. The room had grown dark. I put the lights on in the room and hallway and started packing my things. My body was trembling; I felt as if someone was in the apartment. I went to open the door, then returned to finish packing. Hearing the door creak, I jumped up to see. Then I took a chair and pushed it to block the front door. It crossed my mind that Nadhel might have gone crazy. But no, he was too composed to go crazy. I looked at the coffin, my heart pounding. He was too composed to go crazy. Surely, I was wrong . . . I heard steps approaching. I jumped up to see. A building resident was passing by the door on his way down.

Taking a last look at the coffin, I left. It was only when I reached the building's entrance that I realized that I'd forgotten the key somewhere inside the apartment.

Tangier, 1978

Flower Crazy

The children were raising a ruckus in the neighborhood.

She awoke and sat up, her legs dangling off the edge of the bed. She tilted her head forward. The other two were eating bread dipped in oil and drinking cold green tea that their mother had left in the pitcher. They looked at her as they chewed. The girl was befuddled and dizzy. She held her head in her hands, pressing her fingers to her temples. She got up unsteadily, and still holding a hand to her mouth made for the toilet. Its foul smell made her vomit explosively. Her elder brother handed her a plastic bucket of water. She collapsed back on the bed, sobbing. The younger brother went out into the neighborhood. The older brother was sitting silently in front of her. She sat up. They looked at each other sadly; her eyes dull and tearful. He smiled; they both smiled. With a gesture of her head and hands, she asked him to come over. She seated him next to her. She hugged him to her, smiling, and held his small face in her hands. She wiped away his tears, smiling all the while.

The children in the neighborhood were playing soccer noisily. She gave her brother a coin. He smiled. He kissed her cheek and headed out.

In the neighborhood, misery had grown more familiar

to both young and old. Its beauty peeked out curiously from behind the grim doors. It was the same beauty that was being sold on the streets of the new city.

The crippled neighborhood poet was a witness to all that had happened since the time the local inhabitants had lived in huts.

> He taught the young and the old,
> receiving pay and thanks,
> he read and wrote letters to loved ones,
> he comforted the devastated by reciting the Qur'an,
> he treated those in love with poetry,
> he played with the children,
> he chatted with the elders in the evening.

A small girl was eating a loaf of bread and chocolate, sitting on the doorstep of her house and watching the goings-on in the neighborhood. She was enjoying her food. A child in front of her was holding a red rose, twisting the stem between his thin, dirty fingers. The hunger in his eyes flirted with her loaf of bread. She stopped eating, a morsel of bread held close to her mouth. He was looking at it, smelling it, smiling at it, luring it toward him. Hunger danced in his eyes, his legs, his hands, his whole body. Her dreamy eyes were longing for his dancing rose. His hand stretched toward the mouth and hers toward the nose.

She got up, poured from the pitcher into one of the two oil-smeared glasses, and sipped from the remaining sludge.

She rubbed her eyes and took a gold box of cigarettes from her purse. Sitting on her bed, she lit a cigarette and looked at the picture of her father. She coughed uncontrollably, which reminded her of her father's cough and the streams of blood he used to spit up. Feeling dizzy anew, she got up and headed to the toilet, coughing and throwing away her cigarette. With an effort, she vomited a thin stream of saliva. She recalled the spit of those drunken men—their chatter and violence amid the loud singing and the fog of smoke. She moved toward a small mirror hanging near her bed. Her dark face was turning an olive color. Congested, her eyes dripping, she clasped her hands in front of her. She pressed on the muscles by her clavicle, thrusting her chest forward. Her hands brushed her breasts, and she found them firm. Sitting down on her bed again, she exhaled and stretched her legs, scratching the thick hair that she had not shaved in a long time. She enjoyed her nakedness in her own eyes more than in the eyes of men. Sonnets were recited about her lower body more often than about her upper body.

"The man who was crazy about roses": that was what neighborhood people called him. The crippled poet bore witness to that. The flower-crazy man lived with his mother in a shack. Every morning they'd go together to the city and not return until evening. While she begged, he'd hand out his roses to women and beautiful girls, asking nothing in return. He bought his roses with his mother's money or else stole them. He'd been arrested and tried several times, but because he was crazy about roses, he would be forgiven.

He always threw his last rose to the lady who lived on the ground floor. One day, pitying his obsession with roses, she threw her handkerchief at him. That night he dreamt that he was wildly happy, gathering roses from many rose gardens and showered with handkerchiefs tossed by that woman.

The day of the handkerchief was better than a thousand days. Peace be upon women after that day of the handkerchief. That is what he started saying to everybody he knew. He started registering the story of his life relative to that day: *this happened before the day of the handkerchief; that happened after the day of the handkerchief.* After the handkerchief, even women were not the same. He stopped giving his roses to all the women: the bouquet that he bought or stole was for the handkerchief woman alone. His arrival with the roses and her presence at the window became a promise and a rendezvous between them. When her husband recovered from a cold, he could smell the scent of the man who was crazy about roses on the body of his wife. When he recovered from an eye disease, he watched the crazy man jumping out of the window and saw his wife heading out playfully, chasing the man who was crazy about roses. He was too fat to run after them.

She beautified her night face with makeup, and put blue eyedrops in her eyes. The scent of expensive perfume wafted from her. From her little closet she took out an expensive dress that was transparent, soft, and tighter on her body than all her other dresses, and a pair of beautiful silver high heels. She wrapped them in a piece of paper from a foreign magazine that she had bought to wrap her shoes in, new as well as old. She put on the old shoes and placed the new ones under her arm. Before she left, she cast a look at the large doll in a beautiful dress that she had bought with money she had earned when she was growing up.

Her younger brother was sitting on the doorstep, teasing a kitten with a paper ball tied to a string. A sick dog lay nearby in the shade, exhausted and sleepy. Abandoning the cat, the boy went to bid his sister good-bye. She gave him a coin and a kiss. He told her to come back in the early evening before he went to sleep. Her other brother was playing soccer far away with a group of neighborhood kids. In the street, women and children were drinking from the communal faucet, cursing noisily. A little girl relieved herself near the fence, then poked at her waste with a small stick and smelled it. An emaciated dog hovered near her, its eyes large and tail wagging.

Two girls started a fight about who was first in line for the faucet. One of them pulled up her dress, exposing her naked bottom. "That's what you're worth to me!" she told her rival. The other gave her the middle finger, whereupon they set about punching, tugging, and cursing each other.

Young men were sitting on the ground, backs against the wall, smoking while they watched the goings-on with amusement. One of the young men whistled at her, flirting and laughing, and two children begged her for money. She gave them each a coin and moved on through the mud, embarrassed and miserable. Some of the girls gave her admiring looks, while others were malicious and full of envy.

Near the muddy entrance to the neighborhood, she took

off the old pair of shoes and put on the new ones. She then continued walking along the paved street toward the new city.

The crippled neighborhood poet wrote about those things, and also about things in the city that he had not lived through or seen himself but that he had heard about from people who had been there. Here are a few of his memoirs:

> Yesterday I reevaluated my life in terms of zeros. From right to left, I thought about the value of zeros. I thought about everything by way of nothing. "The Almighty is not to be questioned about what he does, but his followers are to be questioned." Whatever good befalls you comes from God, and whatever bad befalls you comes from yourself. God distributes, and you gather. You are incapable of being just, but God is just. That you ought to destroy all idols: that is what you are able to know. But God will not deceive you if you are to destroy what you have been building for yourselves.

> Sex! Sex! Sex! Here is your misery, so seek the happiness of the promise if you are truly patient and believe. I am angry with this human hunger that does not stop until death. I no longer remember when my pride prevented me from seeking love. Sweet distance was my entire comfort. My promiscuity has always conquered my prudence. I never had the one I desired at the time, the woman whom you would grieve for when she left, yet would feel bored with when she stayed. Beauty! Woe is me for that beauty, the one that devours me but is owned by somebody else who mocks me. I have failed to understand a single woman

except in spontaneous moments of the imagination: in many sips, never in one sip. Perhaps I have thought about all of them. My desires were spread among them. I have not lived the life that I thought I would. Ask the one who lived that life and did not think about it.

It's the confession of the last drink and the last friend who has left me. Ask the one who is in exile. I have a friend who, like me, is vanquished by beauty and who hates me when his wife looks at me, but he doesn't mind when other girls look at me. Ask the one who is bored with the familiar face. Once I had to roam through the sacred house of a woman for three days, and since then I no longer do more than one day in its sunlight or moonlight. The promise of consumption is all the honor of that friend, and I now have some words for the end of the night, for the last drink, for the last cent. I have always hated coercion—who can blame or judge me for that? We are comrades in choice and rivals in coercion.

Single people in this city have become addicted to nightlife and liquor, just like me, or else to repentance and emigration before they turn thirty, fleeing insanity or ignorance and death. Today I am here alone with my drink, like people who run away to bars and brothels, hoping to get something back from the excitement of their celibacy. They glorify liquor in the evening, only to curse it in the morning. Every soul will taste its celibacy, its glory, and its curse. However, in all the brothels I have found my sisters and the sisters of my friends. I have seen the delirium of night melting their makeup, tearing their masks, and riddling their teeth with cavities at the peak of their youth.

I have heard them recall the innocence of their childhood
in school songs, fractured in their memory; in melancholic
novels; in romantic films; and in memories old and recent.

It is the confession of the last drink, the last cent, and
the last friend who travels to a world that I missed visiting at
a time when I had no passport and no money. In the main
street, she entered the bank. She took a check out of her
beautiful, expensive leather bag and signed her name with
difficulty, her hand shaking. The cashier gave her and the
check an inquisitive look. She withdrew two hundred dirhams and left, agitated. Going into a store, she purchased a
women's magazine and a gold cigarette case.

In the tearoom of Mrs. Porte, the pretty waitress approached
her politely. The waitress knew how generous she was.

"Give me orange juice, cold milk, and toast with butter
and jam," she said in a voice shattered by the exhaustion of
the previous night.

In the big market, her mother kept her eye on the guardian who was chasing away street vendors like her.

"Onions! Radishes! Oranges!" she yelled.

In the neighborhood, her brother was playing football.
"Goal!" he yelled.

Her younger brother was playing with the kitten near the
crippled neighborhood poet. The sick dog slumped sleepily
in front of them. A boy, holding a dying sparrow in his hand,
deliberately peed on his shoes by the fence.

Tangier, 1978

The Tent

The Tent

Men Are Lucky

"Always remember that you're a foundling," she told me.

And what about you, I felt like asking her. Who are you? Remember also that I rescued you from your father, who divorced your whore mother. He threatened to kick you out of the house if you didn't marry the first man who asked for your hand. People say that your mother was a whore before and after marrying your father. Today she has become a madam since your father divorced her. How can you be sure that your father is your true father? Can you prove it to me?

But every time we quarreled, I was only trying to explain to her that her existence and mine were simply those of a woman and a man—her and me—about whom we would never know the whole truth, because no one is born the way they wish to be born.

One is born the way others want. And when people become able to think about their own existence, they discover that they have been condemned by others to a life that they must either accept or refuse in their own way. A human being is a human being, regardless of whose son or daughter they are.

"You're such an idiot," she interrupted rudely. "I'm married to an idiot. I don't understand you. You're depraved. Don't forget that you're a foundling."

Blood rushed to my head. I lost the person who, in my imagination, was talking to her. I would beat her over and over until she fainted. Sometimes I would collapse next to her, exhausted, or I'd faint too. Often at night she would wake up several times.

She'd wake me up with a shove.

"Farid!"

"Yes?"

"Wake up!"

"Why?"

"Get up quickly!"

"But why?"

"Someone's trying to break into the house."

"Go back to sleep, Yamna, there's nobody there."

"Listen to that creak."

"It's just the wind shaking the door."

"Coward! Ugh! Are you a man? You aren't a man."

The bitch would keep shaking me, shoving me, uncovering me, and punching me, until I'd get up. Not even once did I ever find anything. And every time, I felt like leaping at her and strangling her. Out of habit, I became afraid of the things *she* feared. In bed she would turn her back on me. A slutty dog's daughter, she always turned her back to me. I would sometimes spend the night staring into the darkness and at the walls. She would often scream or mutter in her sleep. Sometimes when I wanted to make love to her, she would throw me out of the bed. I would detest all women's thighs. At other times, she would call me back into the bed in tears, and that would be my chance to kiss her, hug her, wipe her tears, and make love to her. Or she might leave me to sleep on the hard floor.

"Why am I like this?" she would often ask stupidly. "Why? Why?"

Usually I did not know how to explain her condition.

You're like this, Yamna, I would tell myself, because you're stupid, because you're a bad specimen of humanity, Yamna.

One time, I didn't want to go back to the bed after she had made me leave.

"Stand up and come here!" she started yelling.

"No, I'll stay where I am."

"Get up, I tell you."

"Why? Aren't you the one who made me leave?"

"Seeing you there scares me. You look like a corpse. Come back to bed."

Was I just a corpse, then, in the eyes of this cursed bitch? I was unable to recall any beautiful memories with her.

Is this the woman I'll spend the rest of my doomed life with? I used to ask myself when I felt bored. The woman who won't let me make love to her unless she feels like it?

And even when she does let me, I would muse, making love to her is strange and difficult. She never spreads her thighs. She just lies there, stiff. She keeps her thighs tight as if she were a virgin worried about being deflowered. For such a long time, she wouldn't let me kiss her or touch her breasts.

"I'm not your whore," she'd say. "Go and find a whore whom you can kiss and whose breasts you can touch like that. You're doing what thugs would be doing. Get done quickly and get off me. You're suffocating me; I can barely breathe."

I had complete faith in Doctor Floris. He was a young

man who was very nice to me. The mere thought of him comforted me. Many times I would visit him in my suffering and pain. When I entered his office, my pain would fade. By the time I left, the pain would have totally disappeared, and sometimes I would not need to buy any medicine. One time, I gave her his telephone number.

"What do you want me to do with this piece of paper?" she asked.

"Don't you know numbers?"

"It's none of your business whether or not I know numbers."

Good Lord! You are the one who created everything! I did not believe that she was illiterate even in reading numbers. She looked at the paper in her hand, then threw it on the bed. She looked at me and went into the kitchen.

She's a cow disguised as a human being, I told myself. My sickness made me forget that Yamna was a country girl, ignorant of names and numbers. She used to appear in front of me and then disappear. I imagined her as a child, dirtying her pretty clothes with poo, or an adolescent who'd just menstruated for the first time and didn't know what to do . . . "I've married a most miserable child who can't even count on her fingers."

"This . . . this . . . that . . . that." That was what she would call things whose name she didn't know.

"I don't know," she'd say angrily whenever I tried to teach her the names of things, "and I don't need you to teach me."

"Go, take this paper and ask the grocer to dial this phone number." I was so weak, I'd run out of breath yelling at her. "Get him to ask for Doctor Floris. He'll come to the grocery store; the grocer will bring him here. Tell the grocer that I'm very sick. Go quickly. What are you waiting for?"

She started trembling like me. Her body spasmed, and she burst into tears. She cried and cried until she fell asleep. During the night, I heard her speaking in her dreams, her voice full of lust: "Put it all the way in . . . keep it there . . . put it in . . . put it in . . . !"

We reached Fadan Square. Farid was tired but happy. He trusted me enough to tell me all the details of his life, with no self-restraint—his masturbating, his sex obsession, something from which his marriage to the beautiful Yamna saved him, and about the people who said his mother was Jewish and his father was Moroccan. Before his marriage, he used to ride the crowded bus in the afternoon, when most of the passengers were students. While the bus was moving, he would rub his body against the bum of a girl till he ejaculated. At night, he would masturbate two or three times, sometimes more. He would masturbate to pictures of seminude and nude actresses and singers—I recall Natalie Wood, Elizabeth Taylor, Sophia Loren, Brigitte Bardot, Marilyn Monroe. He also suffered from metaphysical anxiety about death and doomsday.

He showed me his watch.

"What do you think?" he said.

"What?"

"We'll sell it."

"Good idea."

He's become like me, I told myself. I too sold my watch a few days ago, in the flea market in Tangier.

We entered the crowded upper market. I felt an ache inside me and inhaled deeply to ease my exhaustion. I felt nauseated. I drank some lukewarm water from the fountain; it tasted like mucus. We turned right toward El Gharsa Grand Market, where I could smell various kinds of food: fish, bean soup, grilled meat, spices. I inhaled the aromas as I stared hungrily at the items on display in the restaurant windows.

"After we sell the watch," Farid said, "we'll have lunch at one of those restaurants."

My mouth watered, and my stomach longed for any of the food items I could see, or other foods whose aromas were wafting from boiling pots. We mingled with the vendors and customers.

Farid gave his watch to an aged auctioneer.

"Market it well," Farid told him. "I'll pay you more than usual if you can market it well."

The auctioneer had some simple things with him to sell.

"Ten dirhams!" he yelled, raising his hand.

"His voice is weak—faint and hoarse," Farid said. "It won't attract people's attention."

"The people will notice what's in his hand, not his weak voice."

"It seems you don't understand about such things. It's a strong voice that grabs their attention, even if they're asleep."

Bodies moved all around us, cramped and restless. We bumped against them, and at times I felt my foot crushed under someone else's. Sometimes we would apologize and other times we would not. It seemed as if people had nothing to do but be at this damned place.

After half an hour, the auctioneer managed to sell the fine watch for forty-one dirhams. Farid gave him four. Normally, an auctioneer would charge half a dirham for every ten dirhams. The poor man was no dope after all.

I was getting hungrier. I could picture a pan of marinated spiced bean soup, then fried fish and whole-wheat bread. I saw myself squeezing half a lemon onto the fish. My mouth watered for sheer joy, and my eyes misted over. My body shivered, longing for food. We went into a small, miserable restaurant, where a foul stench blended with the smell of spices and food. Three people, exhausted and untidy, were eating, chewing with their mouths wide open. Their teeth were yellow and decayed. They were chewing voraciously, and sucked the head and skeleton of their fish noisily, swallowing in rapid gulps. One of them had an infected eye, like a rotten grape. The hand of another was wrapped in a dirty and bloody bandage. Farid ignored them. Their weathered faces revealed their misery. For just a moment, I thought about the misery of humankind, and a mouthful went down the wrong pipe. Choking, I was afraid I would never breathe again. Farid saved me by thumping my back. The three men looked at me silently while they continued devouring their food. As I took a deep breath and started eating again, I was careful about every bite, chewing it well and swallowing slowly, squeezing the edge of my chair with one hand as I did so. How I despised this soft body of mine! Just thinking about the anguish of swallowing made me suffer before I could actually down my food.

We entered Café Continental, a place I remembered vividly from 1960 and '61. It was not as lively as it used to be. Cafés age too. Now here I was, sitting in an aged café with Farid, who had almost become like the café itself. This one's new paint was like the powder on the face of a woman living on the memories of her youth. We ordered two beers. Farid's silence did not signify anything; it was just dumbness. When a beautiful girl came into the café, he would stare hard at her body. I didn't like it when he tried to relate his troubles to mine. When we were students in Larache, he exploited his orphanhood to practice begging. I'd stand a few steps away while he approached anyone he guessed might give him something. He would put on a show, shrinking his body in a pathetic way, trying to look sick and speaking in a faint, tired voice. When he got what he wanted, his whole personality would immediately shift: eyes sparkling, he would rub his hands together vigorously and strut around, talking confidently . . . What used to annoy me about him, child of vice that he was, was when I would sometimes see or hear him talking with one of them:

"It's for both of us, me and my friend," he would say. "We go to the same school."

I could not stand it when he pointed at me. I would lower my head in humiliation and leave uneasily.

"Why are you so arrogant?" he would ask, chasing after me. "There's nothing shameful about this. We aren't begging."

"What are we doing, then?"

"We're just asking for help because we're poor students; we aren't professional beggars."

But begging for bread wasn't all we did. We used to smoke, and loved black coffee and going to the movies. Sometimes, we would go to the old whores' brothel.

At that point, we didn't have our boarding scholarship yet. Farid was staying at the home of a family who had taken pity on him. They had two young girls who attended the same institute as us. One was a busty girl who was in love with a Moroccan studying in Syria, and the other, with whom Farid was studying math, had a terrible temper. They shared a lop-sided love.

"Salem," he would tell me, "she knows I'm a foundling."

I used to spend half the night at a café. The restrooms had such a foul stench that it hurt the eyes. Sometimes, mice would come up out of the shit hole in the floor and roam through the café, then go back down the hole.

Yamna shoved Farid so hard that he lost his balance.

"Get out of my face," she yelled. "Get out of here, you scum! You drunkard!"

His head hit the wall. As he regained consciousness. I wanted to intervene.

"No, leave us alone," I heard Yamna say to me.

"Yes, stay away," Farid added.

I saw him bend down to grab her legs, with his head under her chest. She was holding him by the waist. I laughed to myself. Truly they were children. So far, I am mine alone. They fell. Now Farid was on top of her, hitting her.

"My face, my face, you slut," I heard him groan, "you're scratching my face. So then, this is how it'll be."

He punched her in the face. Blood dripped from her nose. I heard Yamna's head bang against the door. Farid got up sluggishly, panting.

"That's what this slut wanted! Curse the day I married her."

He sat on the bed, exhausted. I didn't say anything, merely gazed at him in silence. He seemed devoid of any will. I felt my mind go numb. He went into the kitchen. I heard mumbles.

"My head. Just wait. You'll see. Oh, you son of a bitch."

He started sprinkling water on her face while she went on cursing him.

"In a few moments," the conductor said, "we'll be arriving at Rabat Station."

Salem stood in the narrow passage between the two cars. It was his first time riding a train. "This is the first time I'll make love to a woman," he'd told himself a thousand times. "This is the first day I'll smoke and drink. I'll fall in love with a woman who looks like me. I doubt that there's life after death. I'll sleep on the streets like a stray cat on a rainy night . . . I'll get a job. I'll think about suicide. Friendship is false. A thousand beginnings for this and that. Some of them have ended, others have not yet ended, or even started."

I'd found the five-hour trip between Tangier and Rabat long and boring. I'd drunk a small bottle of wine in the train café and smoked a yellow pack of cigarettes. I looked at the scenery—fields and grazing cattle, shepherds and miserable Bedouins. I thought of the Bible, the Qur'an, Beethoven, Michelangelo, and Don Quixote. The headache and emptiness I was feeling in my body were probably caused by the bottle of wine. The squealing brakes grew louder, then the train came to a stop.

A young woman hugged an old man. I might never get such a warm welcome in my life. It's enough that I'm a son who hates his own father. I've no desire to be hater and hated.

He flagged a taxi.

"The Tourist Hotel, please."

At the hotel, he stared at the spots of dirt. When he lifted the bedspread, a foul smell rose from the mattress . . . Apparently, erect candles had melted in a wild extravaganza on this bed. When I lay down. I started feeling itchy. I could imagine blood-sucking insects climbing onto my body, strolling over my skin, and pausing here and there to bite me and suck my blood.

He went out onto the balcony, feeling the urge to scream—but about what? I'd thought the cold night air might be cleansing. Rabat. The Temara neighborhood. A filthy hotel. Insomnia. The suspension of my monthly salary, because of an administrative mistake that had nothing to do with me. Lights and longing. I'm persecuting myself for a reason I don't clearly understand.

Leaving the hotel, he stopped a motorcycle driver. "Please, how do I get to Mohamed V Street?"

"You stopped me for that?" He moved on, cursing.

I felt disappointed. I'm like those shops: dark on the inside and bright on the outside.

He stood in front of a shop display where oranges were arrayed like sleeping breasts. I'm hungry. I love fruit more than meat. The aroma of fruit never makes me feel nauseated; there's no blood oozing out of it. He stood there, watching as four or five dogs circled around a bitch. They were sniffing her behind while she kept trying to fend them off.

He thought back to an incident that had stopped traffic for a few minutes in Tangier. The bitch's crotch had been bleeding, with each drop of blood forming a star on the ground. The spectacle amused the children, but bothered some of the older onlookers who were with their families. The other dogs would run away, then circle back.

"Give them a strong kick and separate them," one man had told the young folk, but no one responded.

Every car made a point of passing by cautiously without harming the canine couple. Salem thought about the painful copulation that dogs endure, which his decorator friend had once explained to him, as naively as a simple-minded gardener might describe his flowers.

Finally, a young hero had appeared, and with a deft kick to the two dogs' backsides, he forced the bloody body parts to separate. They both howled a long sharp bark. As the crisis came to an end, the young onlookers clapped admiringly. Salem went over to the canine couple in pain. The rest of the dogs that had been waiting their turn ran away.

Just like that young hero in France Square, Salem kicked hard. Howls, pain, dogs running away. Yet the copulating couple stayed in place. He felt thwarted. *I will try harder.* He started aiming his leg, but felt unable to move it. Fine then: let them work out a way to separate with the same energy that has kept them coupled.

"Give me anything, sir, may God protect you," a beggar woman said on the Sayyagheen Road.

The young man turned and looked at her. She was cradling a baby in her arms.

"For the sake of my baby daughter," the woman nagged, "give me something for her."

The young man was chatting with another youth . . .

"Why don't you say that to the man who had you spread your legs," he said sarcastically, "making you end up with such a daughter."

The woman was stunned and moved away, sobbing silently.

When Salem continued on, he noticed the dogs making their way back to circle the dog couple. He read the banner on the door of the hotel: Hotel Majestic.

I relaxed. For just a moment, I felt that I was myself again. My exhaustion melted away just like tall candles melting during wild extravaganzas. I fell asleep. Sometimes things become mine once I've thought about them. I once saw a man in Tangier take a lottery ticket out of his pocket. He looked at the list of winning numbers.

"Nothing," he said to his friend.

He took another look at the ticket and put it back in his pocket. "Oh, if only that number was here, and this number was there."

I felt the same way being at Katie's house: like that losing lottery ticket the man had put back in his pocket so sadly. My life's just like those losing tickets, yet I still cling to it. For me, waiting for what will happen has always been less cowardly. Katie is smoking, drinking a beer, and gazing idly at the walls and ceiling. Tick tock. Tick tock. Ten minutes after seven in the evening. March 1967. In mid-March, Julius Caesar was assassinated. On the 30th of March, many Moroccan citizens died in Tangier during a French police shooting. I was born in the month of March. That's what my mother told me, but she didn't remember which day. So I did my own lottery. I wrote the days of the month on scraps of paper. I drew a scrap of paper blindly: March 25th. So that's the day I was born. Ever since that day, I've not felt sad about my lost birthday. I was born at dawn, my mother assured me.

Our hands touched in a blind coincidence, just like picking my birthdate from scraps of paper. It started as a soft, gentle touch, but then things heated up. He could see his small face reflected in her dewy eyes. Her hand was getting warmer and warmer. The warmth of her body drew me closer. Her hands were getting sweaty. Her light mustache became as wet as her hand. I used my tongue to lick the dew on her mustache, and smelled the odor of delicious tobacco mixed with the taste of her lips on mine. She closed her eyes, then opened them, like a dying butterfly. She whispered nothing; just silence. Tick tock. I felt myself in some timeless void. In a single moment, fever struck our bodies. Her eyes twinkled with stars and dew.

He left Katie's house and carried his tiredness to Mohamed V Street. He found himself suddenly facing the warm welcome of the guard's daughter:

"Salem, you're here!"

He had seen her last on the beach of Tangier playing ping-pong.

"What are you doing here?"

"As you can see."

"What about your studies?"

She shrugged her shoulders and frowned. "I got bored with everything in Tangier, so I've moved here to work."

"You've got a job?"

"Not yet," she said. "I'm not alone here. I'm with my friend. She works there," she went on, pointing to a Galerie Paris store. "In just a moment she'll be done with her work. She takes care of the bills."

Samira appeared, short and plump. Dalila introduced her, then flagged a taxi. They all got in.

"Café Brasserie du France," Dalila told the driver.

When they exited the taxi, Salem thought their clothes looked untidy. Maybe they were sleeping in one of the bed-bug hotels, like the first hotel he hadn't slept in the day before. He paid the driver two dirhams, and they entered the café.

"It's been a month and a half since we left Tangier. We've begun to get used to our lives here. The trouble is . . . "

"That's enough, Dalila," Samira cut her off. "Stop worrying. You'll find a job as well."

"I haven't seen your mother since I moved to a different school," Salem told Dalila.

The waiter appeared. Dalila asked for a beer, Samira asked for a coffee with milk, and Salem also ordered a beer.

"But did your mother agree to your coming here with Samira?"

"I won't allow anyone to interfere with my life anymore," Dalila said. "She was wearing me out with her advice. When I realized she wanted to get rid of me, I couldn't bear her any longer. She told me that a very rich man wanted to propose to me.

"'Be reasonable, Dalila,' she told me. 'Wear this kaftan. Don't let people hear us quarreling. The man's going to come this evening.'

"'No, I won't wear that kaftan,' I screamed in her face. 'You wear it. It suits you better than me.'

"'Be reasonable,' she said. 'You'll serve tea to the man and his family. Give him a chance to get a good look at your face. You're beautiful. Be charming when presenting the tea and sweets, and be demure. Keep calm; the man is from an aristocratic Tangier family, conservative and honorable. Don't disgrace us in front of fine people.'

"'Why should I care if the man's from a Tangier family, conservative and honorable?' I yelled at her. 'No. I'm still too young. I'm not even sixteen yet. I don't know this man, and I don't want to know him. Tell him to look for a girl from a conservative and honorable family from Tangier like his own.'"

Dalila stopped talking.

"Did you see the man who wanted to propose?" he asked her.

"No. I ran away that evening and stayed with Samira. Next morning, we came here."

Samira sat there, her hands on her knees, smiling intermittently. She gave Dalila a loving, admiring glance . . . I smiled gently at Samira.

"She's right," she said bitterly. "Similar trouble was waiting for me too. These days, most parents are like that. It's best to move away as soon as you can."

"If I don't find a job here," Dalila said confidently, "Samira and I can move to Casablanca. It's a city with a good job market."

The three of them left the café, where they were met by a cold snap. Salem hailed a taxi.

"Star Cinema," Dalila told the driver.

At the theater entrance, he realized that dozens of eyes were watching our movements. It was predominantly a cinema for men; we saw only a handful of women. He stood between Dalila and Samira and gave a thousand francs to Dalila. She was leading our little group, and insisted on buying the tickets herself. It was a local cinema, like Tangier's Kazar or Capitol or American.

Samira seemed more mature than Dalila, even though

she was Dalila's age or perhaps younger. Dalila did not give him back the change. He did not catch the title of either of the films that were going to be screened, one after the other.

Inside, Salem was dozing off when suddenly he heard Samira yelling at the guy sitting next to her.

"If you don't leave me alone, I'm going to call the police!"

Someone sitting behind them tapped Salem on the shoulder.

"Hey!"

A glass of wine. So here, too, people shared wine from the same glass, just as they did in the Kazar and Capitol cinemas in Tangier. He was going to refuse the glass. Gunshots and screams of Red Indians on the screen were mixed with screams from the audience.

"Here comes the second film, the good one." Dalila said, nudging him with her elbow.

After the films, fatigue robbed him of any desire.

At first, Salem had found Samira desirable. He did not feel the same way about Dalila.

"Taxi!" Salem yelled.

He no longer felt like spending the rest of the night with them. They lived with another two women in a single apartment. Samira sat calmly beside him.

"I feel the cold more in Rabat than in Tangier," Dalila said.

Salem noticed the way Samira's legs moved. She was a chestnut-haired brunette, her face as round as an apple, her breasts like two eggs.

The girls got out of the car, and he went on to his hotel. The streets were deserted.

Nights in Rabat are different from those in Tangier, he thought. At this hour, people would be walking along the boulevard and in the Petit Socco.

He always adored the morning sun. He hadn't slept well. As he peered out the window of the speeding car, people's faces passed by him like trees. They looked more tired than the faces of people in northern cities. Here I feel overwhelmed by this city, which I am visiting for the first time.

"Which do you prefer, sunrise or sunset?" he had once asked his friend Karima at the Kankas bar early one morning.

She was surprised.

"I've never thought about it before," she replied, like a confused child.

"Try thinking about it," he said. "Then tell me which you find more beautiful."

He met her several times after that, and each time he repeated the same question, jokingly. Each time, her answer was the same.

"One day, I'll try," she would respond seriously.

"Start this evening," he would tell her. "If you try, I'll give you a beautiful gift."

"Not today. One day I'll try. I don't like being told what to do."

From afar, he could see Samira stacking clothes on a vending cart.

They said good morning.

"I'm going back to Tangier," he told her.

"Won't you stay with us another day?"

"I can't. Tomorrow I have to be at work."

"I wanted to tell you something important—but what was it? I forget so much these days."

She placed a finger on her cheek.

"Oh, now I remember!" she said. "Don't tell Dalila's mother that you saw us here," then added, "Come back to us someday."

"What about Dalila, where's she today?"

"I left her sleeping."

He smiled at her and said good-bye. She waved. He remembered what his friend Aziz had once told him:

"Sometimes, the feeling of true love is like when you're traveling in a train, and the girl you love is traveling on a different train going in the opposite direction."

He turned to her one last time. Her smile looked forlorn.

I realized that she was not happy about the pregnancy, but she didn't want to hide the bulge in her belly.

"Get an abortion if you don't want it," I suggested.

"Do you want me to end up in hell?" she replied. "Do you think I'm like you? I'm no criminal."

The fetus was imposing itself upon us more and more, day by day. It was growing, and I kept telling myself: another problem. His screaming would disrupt the quiet and clear moments inside this house. He will not be any different from all the annoying babies in this world. How I hate screaming babies! However, I know that screaming is the only way babies can express themselves.

A week after the birth, I found a piece of paper covered

in primitive handwriting, misshapen letters that did not stay on the line. I showed her the piece of paper. She threw it down and began trembling.

"Keep that away from me. Where did you find it?"

I picked it up.

"I found it tucked into the folds of the sofa."

"Take it out of the house. No, keep it. We'll look for someone who can cancel its effect. Really, only evil magic can undo evil magic."

She started sobbing, hugging the child. She kissed him and caressed his head gently.

"Damn all envious women," she said. "Damn me, too! I wish I'd been born a man! You men are lucky in everything. It's we women who have to put up with all your worries."

After making a dizzying, uncertain effort, I finally managed to understand that she thought a sterile woman must have created this spell to rob her of her fertility and make her barren. I explained to her that it was just some verses from the Qur'an, written confusingly and full of mistakes. There was nothing about infertility or fertility or having to do with spells. Even so, she stuck to her delusions. Taking some money, she went to look for a magician to undo the spell's effect.

"Powerful enchantment can be reversed only by a powerful enchanter," she kept repeating, anxiously and fearfully.

"Farid?"

"Yes?"

"Get up."

"Why?"

"Devils are fighting inside my soul. Damn me that I married a man like you, afraid of his own shadow."

After the shock of the spell, she started having violent temper tantrums. She kept on asking for forgiveness for some delusional sins she had never committed.

"What did I do, God? I'm innocent. They want to do me evil. Save me from them! You're the only one who knows my agony."

"Farid?"

"Yes?"

"Read me a sura from the Qur'an. Reading the Qur'an will certainly comfort me. Read me a chapter. I'm miserable."

I read her a chapter or two.

"And now?" I said after finishing my reading.

"I feel better now."

For hours, her sharp, intermittent wailing blended with the baby's screams.

"I married a sick and foolish woman," I mused. "I'm going to end up sick and foolish like her.

"Neither of us even wanted the child. What exactly made me marry her? I don't know. Probably I was out of my mind, desperate to find the girl of my dreams, disgusted by my masturbation routine. Sex! That is the problem, Salem. Sometimes we would fight, and the baby would cry."

"Enough!" I screamed in her face one day. "You win!"

We faced each other. We were both out of breath, pathetic and stupid.

Do you want to keep going? her eyes asked me.

No. I told you, you've won, I told her in my imagination.

I divorced her. It was the only solution. Her father visited me. I was out at the café watching TV: Muhammad Ali Clay beating an English opponent. Her father was waiting for me in front of the house. He said we needed to talk. When we entered the house, I asked him to sit, but he refused. I spotted evil in his eyes.

"Why did you hit my daughter?" he demanded. "Talk to me, you son of a bitch, you bastard."

He didn't wait for me to explain. Instead, he attacked me, and we started hitting each other ferociously. He kept biting me and cursing me in a rural dialect that I didn't understand. When we'd exhausted ourselves, we sat on the bed.

"I'll kill you, you son of a bitch," he said. "You don't know country people yet. I could see evil in your eyes from the first day you came asking to marry my daughter. Lots of people told me I'd be an idiot to let her marry a foundling like you. Everyone knows you're a foundling, brought up in an orphanage. God wouldn't bless such a union. However, I pitied you and thought that it didn't matter. I told myself it was enough that he was a man who wanted to be like other people, that he was a Muslim and a Moroccan. Some people told me that your mother didn't have a fixed religion. I didn't believe them, but today I believe everything that was said about you, you animal. You ruined my daughter's youth, then divorced her. Now she's turned into a prostitute on the streets."

Children and women had gathered by the door. Blood

was dripping from his mouth. I was scratched on my face and neck, with bites on my shoulder, arm, and back. Some of his bites had taken off skin. He'd tried to grab my balls. What saved me was a head-butt I had given him in the face. While he was reeling, I hit him twice in the stomach. He curled up and hit the ground.

"And Yamna, where is she now?"

"I don't know. Maybe she's at her father's place or selling her body on the streets."

"And the child?"

"I gave up my rights to her."

Farid's voice was weary, and the pain in his stomach was severe. He uncovered his belly, which was covered with brown freckles.

"What's that?" I asked him, surprised.

That is another story. I was sick. My neighbor al-Qadiri visited me, accompanied by a religious cleric. I explained to them that I do not believe in cures by phony clerics. Al-Qadiri was furious; he considered my words disrespectful to both him and the cleric. For just a moment, they looked at each other silently.

What do they want with me? I wondered.

Suddenly they pounced on me and tied my hands behind my back. When I started screaming, they gagged my mouth. Yamna brought in a fire pot with sparks flying from it, and the son-of-a-bitch cleric took the red-hot skewer and started pressing it to my skin and spitting on my burns. The smell of my burning skin was suffocating me, and I started to vomit and pee in my pants. He was delighted to be burning me—I could see it in his foxy eyes. He recited some mysterious spells while al-Qadiri, the bastard, nodded his head approvingly.

"Carry on, God bless," I heard him say. "Everything's fine."

"He's responding well to the therapy," the fox said.

My head was filled with insane screams, and my heart was pounding violently.

"Be reasonable, Mr. Farid," al-Qadiri told me. "Just a few more moments, and everything will be fine. You are in the presence of a man whose blessings are greater than the treatment of a thousand doctors. Oh, if only you realized in whose presence you are now."

The impostor continued assuredly searing my stomach. Despite being tied by my wrists, I tried in vain to escape al-Qadiri's clutches. He was holding me down as hard as he could.

"Show some of Jacob's 'beautiful patience.' Curse the devil and calm down; let's save your life. As God is our witness, we don't want to hurt you."

Help! Help! I screamed in my imagination.

"We understand your condition. We don't blame you, Mr. Farid. Be reasonable. You are in the hands of the very best people. His blessings are gifted from God and from His saints."

When the impostor had finished his treatment, al-Qadiri removed the gag.

"I'm going to kill you both later," I said in a weak voice.

"It's a shame you talk like that in front of this good man," al-Qadiri chided me. "I don't care if you insult me; but you should respect this honorable man."

He untied me. I tried to kick the impostor, but missed the son of a bitch.

"Damn you," I said feebly.

"Whatever is God's will will be, Mr. Farid," al-Qadiri said. "You've never been like this before."

I was dizzy and had difficulty breathing. I wanted to spit at them, but I was afraid they would think I needed an even stronger treatment than the one they had just given me.

I visited Doctor Floris. He prescribed some medicine for my frayed nerves, and an ointment for my burnt, ulcerated belly.

Later, Salem and I visited the Rebertito pub.

"You need to give up your usual habits before you collapse again," Salem said.

"You know I fear sexually transmitted diseases. I used to masturbate once or twice a week, even when I was married to Yamna. When I was having sex with her, I used to visualize another woman. Who can be married to Yamna and not masturbate?"

"Do you know the woman who runs that house?" Salem asked as he pointed at a building we were nearing.

"No."

"Let's go over. Maybe she's there."

"Who?"

"The Lady Shama. I know her."

Lady Shama opened the door.

"So I thought you might be here, Lalla Shama," Salem said.

"And where do you think I'd go?" she replied. "And you,"

she said to me as she shook our hands, "are you still in Tangier?"

"Yes."

"And the Petit Socco, is it still inhabited by hippies?"

"Where do you think they'd go?"

"Even here in Tétouan, they've started swarming like locusts, moving into the suburbs and poor neighborhoods."

"They like the simple life."

"But they're dirty. Hippie women infect our young men with sexual diseases."

"They aren't all sick, Lalla Shama."

"They're very dirty. Men and women alike. Dirtiness causes illness. A woman who sleeps with a man and doesn't wash afterward will get sick and infect whoever sleeps with her later."

"That's true."

Lady Shama looked as happy as always. A young girl was standing nearby, smoking. She gave them both a cold stare. Farid let Salem deal with Lady Shama, and moved a few steps away from them.

"There's another girl taking care of a customer," Salem said to Farid. "You go ahead with this one, and I'll wait for the other one."

"You go first," Farid replied. "I'll wait for the other girl."

"I don't mind. Why don't you go with this girl? She's attractive, don't you think?"

"It's better if you go first."

"Okay, let's play heads or tails. Whoever wins gets to go first."

Lady Shama laughed as she looked at the girl, who now came over.

"They're going to flip a coin for you," Lady Shama said to her. "This is the first time I've seen that in my life."

Salem tossed the coin in the air, then caught it in his right hand and immediately slapped it onto the back of his left.

"Heads or tails?"

"Tails," Farid said with a smile.

"Heads." Salem lifted his hand.

"Bring me a beer," Farid said to Lady Shama and plunked himself down on a chair.

Salem followed the girl to her room. Her smile reminded him of an Irish girl he'd once known in Tangier.

"Your friend seems sad."

"That's the way he is."

Lady Shama entered the room carrying a tray with two beers.

"The other girl my friend's waiting for, is she done yet?" Salem asked her.

"I heard the door of her room opening. That means that the man who was with her is about to leave."

Salem thought of his friend Salwa. Maybe when I head back, I will find her in Tangier. She really likes ice-cold beer and Lucky Strike cigarettes.

"When I spend summers in Meknes and winters in Marrakesh," I'd once heard her tell her friend Afaf, "I thrive and get plump. But in Tangier, I lose weight no matter the season."

Salwa's life is completely tied to her vagina's health.

"You seem preoccupied."

The girl handed him his drink.

"Sorry," he said with a smile, "that's how I am sometimes."

He looked at her face, the way her lips moved.

She's really nice, he thought.

She'd finished her drink and started undressing. I must learn to shed my sadness as easily as she takes off her clothes. How I wish I could have prevented what happened to Salwa with that merchant.

"How much is this skirt?" she'd asked him.

"I don't sell things to drunk people in the morning. It's bad luck. Get out of my store."

"I'm here to shop. It's none of your business whether I'm drunk or not. Tell me the price."

"Leave."

"A fish seller will always be a fish seller. From a fish seller in Larache to a clothes merchant in Tangier who despises his customers."

"Get out of my store."

"I won't. Tell me the price of this skirt so I can take it."

"Take it then."

He slapped her hard. Not a single bystander interfered. I wanted to go to her aid.

"Stay where you are," one of them said. "Don't get involved in what doesn't concern you. Are you her guardian?"

They encouraged the merchant to beat her.

"Give it to her!"

"More!"

"She deserves worse!"

"He is a devout and respected merchant!"

"She's a drunken whore!"

"We'll testify for him!"

Her nose was bleeding.

"Do you all see? She came to me, this damn bitch, and bothered me. I won't conduct business with drunkards, but she acted like a frenzied bitch. She insulted me and my entire family."

"Yes, you're right. We're with you!"

"She sleeps around with Europeans in the boulevard hotels," one of them said. "I know some of the Christians that she's escorted."

"Indeed, she's a bitch."

"We don't even know where she came from."

"She's sluttier than a chicken, as the Spaniards say."

A policeman appeared.

"Take her away, the rotten scum," he said roughly.

The group was too disgusted to pick her up, so they just dumped her on the ground. Her eyes were wide open, her nose bleeding with red mucus, and her clothes torn.

"Drag her. She's just pretending."

Two men carried her by the armpits, her head sagging forward. When they neared the police station, a drunken old man yelled scornfully at the security men:

"Move back! You all know who she is. You all saw what happened to her. What are you waiting for now? Go look for something else!"

Salem started to roam over the girl's body. He thought of *La Maja Desnuda*, feeling weightless. The wild soft mouth opened, closed, and started sucking his penis.

When he emerged from the room with the girl, Lady Shama looked upset.

"Your friend left with the other girl," she told him.

"How did that happen?" he asked, surprised.

"Ask him. I don't know."

"Did poor Yamna go with him?" the girl asked Lady Shama gently.

"Yes, she went with him," Lady Shama responded scornfully, then pointed at Salem. "Tell Salem that he can take you with him too if he wants."

The girl laughed, giving Salem a passionate look. He sat down on the chair and asked Lady Shama for a beer.

Tangier, March 1967

The Three Mouths

I walked silently beside her. She glanced at me without saying anything. I'll tell her how much I'll pay. I'd seen her in the square, but had not talked to her before. I used to know almost all of them. When I'm old, will I still have a few qualities left so I can have a woman?

"For women," an old man once told me, "the advantage of old men is money, whereas the advantage of young men is pleasure."

I can already feel the humiliation of aging with no money. It scares me. Maybe that's why my desire for this girl is like that of someone visiting a cemetery in order to feel alive. We turned toward Fez Street.

"Are you free at the moment?" I whispered.

She gave me an indifferent look. I realize she's heard that question a hundred times before, but what is a man supposed to say to a professional woman?

"Do you want to spend some time together?"

"I'm sorry. I only have fifteen minutes before I have to go to work in the Randy Winston disco."

I looked at my watch: 9:45 p.m. She went into the small café close to the disco. I stepped back as she entered, then sat down beside her.

The waiter placed a cup of espresso in front of her. I ordered a cold beer. Under her eyes were two bruises that her rosy makeup could not conceal. Almost all of them had patrons.

"We can be quick," I suggested, "at a nearby hotel."

Just then a young, beautiful, black Moroccan girl entered.

"Alice, here you are," she said. "I've been looking for you."

As the waiter gave me my beer, the two girls kissed each other on the cheeks. The second girl greeted me with a nod. She too was a professional; I had seen her in the prostitutes' corner on the square. She and Alice chatted a bit, then the black girl got up and sauntered over to the counter. She exchanged a friendly look and quick laugh with the waiter, who was also black. She ordered black coffee and came back to sit with us. She seemed worried. She examined some bumps that covered her limbs and scratched her left arm.

"Did you get a blood test?" Alice asked.

"Not yet," she replied, taking a puff from her cigarette. "Redouan told me that it's just a skin rash."

She uncovered her thighs, which were covered in blisters.

The waiter placed her cup of coffee in front of her.

I once saw a classmate of mine, from the city of Larache, urinating blood. He would walk with his legs apart. He looked pale and moved sluggishly. When he pointed out the girl who'd given him the infection, I bet him that I could sleep with her without getting the disease. At that time, I thought that every illness was connected to willpower, strong or weak. I knew nothing about infectious diseases.

When I got the feeling that the black girl was about to leave, I got up quickly and went to the toilet, to avoid shaking hands with her. I left the toilet cautiously, trying to think

of an excuse to go back to the toilet, or to leave the café alto-
gether, if she was still there. I returned to my seat.

"I'll give you fifteen hundred francs, I promise you," I
said to Alice, desire blazing in my eyes. "Fifteen minutes,
no more."

She smiled as she sipped her coffee.

These professional women, I thought, they seem to like
this flirty game. They're remembering their lives before they
turned pro.

I pictured an ox smelling the ass of a cow, raising its head
to the sky and inhaling the cow's scent in its nostrils. Then it
would go *Mooooo* . . . If the cow walked away, the raging ox
would follow her . . .

"Maybe tomorrow," she said. "I only woke up an hour
ago, and had dinner half an hour ago. I need to get over to
the disco now."

I paid the waiter for the coffee and beer, and I, the ox, followed the cow to the barn.

"Write me all about your sexual encounters these days . . . "
That's how my friend Ahmed from Tétouan concluded his last
letter to me.

"I'm drafting this letter after my last encounter," I write to
him now. "Hours ago, the perfume of a woman was making
me dizzy. The reason I'm staying in Tangier is that a curse
compels me to do so—a curse, yet it's sweet. If you were here
with me, we would both have ejaculated the crazy living
sperm in the same sticky, fleshy cave. The strongest of desires turns into bitter impotence when the situation evokes
the slightest disgust. The roots of this experience are rotten.

I'm no longer pure. I've fallen into this rotten reality. Yours faithfully, Idris."

I had already written to him about my experience with Nora a year before. I didn't know what I wanted from her. I'd met her at the end of the month. I was used to splurging for just one day after I received my monthly paycheck: one day, and then I was broke again. I went with her to the Hotel Goya. She had a toothache, and I was exhausted. As she undressed, I smoked to calm my nerves. Fear of failure made me tremble. I paid her two thousand francs in advance, so she wouldn't worry. She lay down on the bed, reassured and glowing. I was worried that she might have syphilis, perhaps because of a book I'd recently read about sexual relationships. Shaking, I spread her thighs with my hands. I smelled her vagina. The scent of a dead animal rushed to my nose, and I felt nauseous.

"What is it?" she asked, upset. "Do you think I'm dirty?"

I could visualize her innards and bladder bubbling.

"No," I replied. "Not at all. You aren't dirty."

"Then why are you sniffing me like that?"

We were silent.

"Are you going to start or not?" she asked. "If you don't feel like it now, then just let me go. We'll meet some other time."

"Don't be upset," I replied, suppressing my nausea so that I wouldn't throw up on her. "When I feel tired, the act of smelling gets me horny."

"But I don't want someone who sniffs my thighs," she said. "Couldn't you choose something to sniff other than my thighs? I'm not dirty or sick. It seems to me that you're the one who's sick."

I moved away from her and took the condom out of my

pocket. I couldn't put it on: I wasn't erect yet. Her vagina gaped open, and my penis hung limp. The condom was in my hand, and I could feel the bile from my sour stomach rising in my throat. What would she say about me when she went to gossip with her friends in the profession?

"Nora, let's flip the shoe," I said.

"Aha!" she responded. "You want to do that with me? Why didn't you say that to begin with? For just two thousand francs, you want me to agree to do anything you want?"

"I'll add another thousand francs."

She did not respond, but turned onto her stomach. She seemed to be accustomed to this. Her behind was brown, round, a little boy's ass. This was my last chance with her. But I was still limp.

"Enough," she said. "You aren't the first to be in this situation. You must be very tired, or maybe you're in love with another girl."

"That's right," I said, getting off her timidly, "I'm tired. But I'm not thinking about anyone except you."

When women feel frigid, they do not get ashamed the way men do. For us, an erection is our manhood. Women just keep their secret in their caves.

She got up, naked, and went to wash. I stayed in bed. When she turned to face me, her breasts were small, her nipples brown and erect. She was beautiful from both back and front. She removed a bottle of nice perfume from her purse and dabbed her neck, her armpits, and her chest. I asked her for the bottle and perfumed my face to get rid of the traces of that imagined smell, which was still there in my nose. As she was putting her clothes back on, I took out four thousand francs and extended them to her.

"Try with me one last time with your tongue."

She grabbed the money but didn't say anything right away.

"At least go wash up," she said finally, smiling.

Naked, I got up and went to wash. She stretched out on the bed, resting her head on her hands.

"Better save this for another time," I said.

"Yes, that's best."

We left the hotel and headed for the Madame Brot tea hall. We ordered Alexandra cocktails. She asked me to write three letters for her, to three men who lived in Casablanca, Rabat, and Meknes.

"They've told me what you're doing there with dirty prostitutes," she dictated to me for her friend Nizar in Meknes. "And I know what I'll do with you when I get there."

She suggested that we go to the Tajada cabaret. On the way, I apologized for annoying her at the hotel. She told me that some kind of obsession had taken hold of me. When I told her she was beautiful, she laughed and said I was a liar. In the cabaret, the belly dance show had started. I was drinking, and went to the bathroom to empty my bladder. She left me all alone, and I saw her dancing with a stylish young man. They ordered drinks on my tab. I couldn't protest. I was desperate to have some kind of relationship with her.

By four in the morning, I realized I had spent more than half my month's salary. I left the cabaret drunk, cursing myself and the world. I wandered the streets searching for another professional woman I could sleep with, someone who could save me from my supposed impotence.

I remembered the day I asked her to marry me on Atlas Beach.

"I'm being trained now," was what she told me that day. "When I finish . . . Oh, I can't promise you anything. Look for some other girl to marry."

I was on sedatives to calm my nerves. Maybe my weakness and loneliness were what explained my desire to be attached to her. I was looking for a nurse, not a wife.

Alice approached us.

"It was Alice who told me that you work here as a belly dancer," I told Nora.

"Have a drink with us," Nora said to Alice.

"Later," she replied, and left.

"What's her real name?" I asked Nora.

"Rashida. Why do you ask? Are you planning to fall in love with her?"

"Love comes without consideration," I replied with a laugh. "She's nice."

"I've matured," she said after a moment's pause. "I'm not the person you used to know."

"Is that so? Are you wiser today than that night we got drunk together at the Tajada cabaret?"

She laughed. That was what I liked about her. She faced up to things as if their only purpose was to entertain her.

"How did you spend the rest of that night?" she asked.

"I went to my hotel and slept like an animal."

I vividly recalled that next morning. I was like a child, threatened by my impotence. Maybe that was because I loved her before I desired her. That is what had happened to me with Rhimou al-Roubia before her as well.

"Ramia told me that you went with her the next day to

the same hotel," she said. "You asked for the same room, to sleep with her."

"True."

"Why?"

"It's a secret."

"You're weird," she said, then went on, "I'm going to the dressing room now to change."

She got up and disappeared. I thought about Ramia. I desire you, Ramia. I don't fear anything about you. You are more tender and beautiful than frigid Nora. My failure with her that night was not about me specifically. Maybe at that point, Nora had been thinking about her other lovers in distant cities.

A tall, elderly woman entered, followed by Rubio and, behind them, Samir, the singer.

"What's this?" Samir yelled. "Do I really see Farida before me?"

I looked at the woman who was sitting to my right with a handsome young man. She shook hands with Samir warmly.

"Where have you been?" he asked her.

"I was in London," the woman said merrily. "From Madrid, I went to London,"

The tall woman and Rubio sat at Farida's table. Her lips were what I always dreamt of in a woman's face. Kisses are an exchange of germs; medical diagnoses always dull my sexual lust. For a long time, I dreamt about the face of this woman returning from London, a woman whom I had never seen before.

"If you don't sing 'Blue Eye' well tonight," Farida told Samir, "I'm going to throw this glass at you."

She took a drink from her glass. Samir made mocking gestures, sneering and screwing up his face. Farida giggled.

The woman returning from London was amused. The room started to fill up with people.

"You're here, too," Samir said, looking at me.

He sat between me and the woman. He introduced me to her and her friend.

"We worked together at one of the discos in Madrid," he told me in his theatrical accent. "I played drums for her. Farida and Badia work at the Kutoubia disco and are the best dancers in Tangier. Their bodies are made of bronze."

"Enough, Samir!" Farida said with a laugh. "Have a drink with me."

Samir waved to the waiter and ordered an empty glass.

"Once, at the Hamra disco, the belt that holds her dancing outfit came loose. She was performing the Eve in the Jungle dance. But she didn't leave the stage. The lights dimmed, and she continued to dance. Ha, ha, ha!" he concluded.

The waiter brought the glass, and Farida filled it from the bottle of whiskey on her table. He drank his glass in one gulp and got up.

"Now I'll get ready to sing," he said, and left.

"Jerry, I left the box of cigarettes in your bag," Rubio told the elderly woman gruffly.

This Rubio's a child, I thought.

She extended her hand to the bag on the table, but it fell on the ground.

"You're never careful when you touch things," Rubio commented childishly.

The woman apologized gently and bent over to pick up the bag.

"Leave that to me," Rubio said angrily. "I'll kill everyone for your sake, but only if I see you calm down."

"Rubio, be respectful," Farida said. "You're being rude."

"I was just joking with her," Rubio laughed.

"That's not joking."

I noticed Nora come out of the dressing room. She was beautiful in a red Moroccan kaftan. She blew me a kiss. Her gestures reminded me of a cow moving her head or tail to chase flies away. She stopped at the bar near three men. The Moroccan musicians had started to pluck the strings of their instruments. The oud player launched into a little melody. Samir got close to the microphone and began a Lebanese tune, imitating Fahd Ballan.

"Now, ladies and gentlemen," he said as the music paused, "we're going to present to you 'Blue Eye.' I'm going to ask our colleague Farida, the famous dancer, who is here with us tonight, to come up and dance to this folk song."

The loud rhythm now started. Farida jumped up on the stage, barefoot. She looked like Salome balancing John the Baptist's head on a tray.

Alice came over.

"Don't blame Nora for the way she treats you here," she whispered. "She has to distribute her kisses to all the men who invite her for a drink."

"I didn't say a word," I told her with a smile. "Do you two have a lesbian relationship?"

"You're evil."

Farida came over to us, still dancing. She was melting with sweetness. The audience looked in our direction, totally absorbed. I wanted to tell Farida to take those laughing eyes somewhere else, but I did not dare. I couldn't mouth even a single one of the thousand words I had in mind. Alice took a drag on her cigarette, inhaling with pleasure. Farida bestowed her smiles on the young men, then led them away coquettishly. A drunk man pulled her toward him, and she went along. He kissed her belly. She moved away. I imagined an ox smelling the behind of a disgusted cow. The room reverberated with laughter and lustful comments. Farida's young friend looked at her, annoyed. I looked at Jerry. Her body looked like a dead tree; she was leaning her head on the shoulder of her young lover. Samir was a good singer. The musicians were lively with their instruments, like puppets; in hoarse voices they kept chanting parts of the chorus along with Samir. They cleared their throats before singing their verses. The escort ladies of the disco surrendered to their customers' kisses. Everyone was having a good time, time that I conceived as a huge barrel, their gaiety leaking from a hole in the bottom. The swamp of time around the barrel reeked.

Samir finished singing.

"Belly dance!" a voice shouted.

"Yes, belly dance!"

"Belly!"

"Belly!"

"Belly!"

The band resumed playing an oriental melody, and Samir, sweaty, came over to sit by my side.

"Farida will fulfill their secret desires tonight," he said. "I swear to you, most of them will pleasure themselves to her dances, even if they already have a woman at home."

He poured a glass of whiskey. Farida moved quickly to her table, following the rhythm, and downed her glass in one shot while still dancing. She then danced away again, a smile on her face like a split pomegranate. Her body was heating up, as though struck by a fever. She imposed herself on the customers, who forgot who they were in her presence. I too enjoyed every gesture she projected into the air.

One of the disco escort ladies passed in front of me.

"Come and have a drink," I said.

"I'm already taken for now. Afterward, I can come to you, and keep drinking with you till morning if you like."

"Her name's Jamila," Samir said.

"Do you know her?"

"I know all of them. She's from Tétouan."

"I've never seen her before."

"She's new as a professional. She's only attracted to men for their money. She prefers older men to younger ones. The young ones soil her thigh and don't pay her enough even to bathe in a public bath. Sometimes they treat her roughly."

Farida was flying as she danced. Everyone there was trying to catch the fish in the pond. As she reached the climactic moment in her dance, she moved closer to the drummer and undulated her belly rapidly, as if a rabbit was madly trying to kick its way out. It was trapped inside her stomach, out of breath. The drumbeats now became slower and quieter, like a pulse in a dying body. The onlookers' mouths drooped open. The trapped rabbit struggled. It was getting ready to escape, leaping, running away. Amazed eyes were blinking; even as they returned to their senses, they were still chasing the rabbit inside Farida's belly. The music came to a close. The delicious warmth turned cold. Farida waved her hands in the air, bowing this way and that. Applause and cries of admiration arose as she extended her arms to the audience. I felt my senses bleeding.

That woman has a rabbit trapped inside her stomach, I

mused. She has the skill to make people lose their minds over her rabbit until she decides to give them their minds back.

Now I see Nora in the arms of a man. My feelings are all over the place. I desire and do not love; I love and do not desire. I feel jealous about someone I do not wish to possess. I want something, not for its own sake, but for what it can provoke in other people, which I would enjoy watching. I see Nora going into the dressing room. Farida is talking with her admirers. The musicians are tuning their instruments. Samir is talking to Jamila. I called to him, and he came over, laughing loudly.

"Is it Nora's turn?" I asked him.

"Yes."

"Jamila doesn't dance?"

"She doesn't know how to dance, even in bed. She feels naked when she stands in front of an audience. She's only pleasing from a distance. She's just a body. This is her first week in the disco. In Tétouan she was married. It's said that her husband found her making love with a woman, so he divorced her. On her first day here, she seemed like an orphan child. She sat in the corner of the hall, taking everything in. I waited to see what would happen between her and the guests.

"'Go and get that doll to move,' the disco's boss said to me, 'or I'll have to fire her.'

"'If you want to keep a job here,' I told her, 'you need to move in front of the guests.'

"'What do you want me to do with them?'

"'Flirt with them. Use all the stupid things you know to make them laugh. Stroke their beards. When they're with women, they're just grown-up children.'

"'Don't be scared,' I went on. 'They're men during the day and children at night. They're only men when they're fighting over a woman. When you tell them a joke, slap their butts with your hand. Some of them will only laugh at jokes if you have a finger in their butt. Pull their hair. Gently nudge their crotch. Sometimes that's how their sexual desires are aroused. They love that.'

"We laughed. From that day, she turned into an animated doll."

Samir went to the bar to entertain some anxious customers.

Farida came over. "I see you're dozing off," she said.

I sat up.

Making other people happy makes her younger and more beautiful, I thought.

In her eyes I could see a double-sided mirror.

"Have a drink with us," she said.

Lifting the whiskey bottle, she poured a glass. Her movement, the color of the drink, the way it swirled in the glass, reminded me of the faces of all the women who had ever filled my glass.

Her young friend's look was frozen. He sat there silently as the band played some oriental dance tune.

Nora's a human cobra, I told myself. She'll be coming out of the dressing room to entertain people.

Now I saw Nora, the cobra, emerge. She was wearing a red-gold dress and throwing smiles at the guests. Some of them winked at her, others smiled back; still others kept on talking and laughing, paying her no attention. Her father was an alcoholic. When she lost her virginity, he tried to kill her. His death marked a new chapter in her life as a dancer.

She was shaking and shimmying like a fruitless tree.

"She's amazing," Farida said.

Nora smiled at everyone, moving her hands like an Indian temple dancer.

Even her dance is mysterious, I thought.

She was twisting her lower body and moving her belly in quick thrusts. All of a sudden, she froze.

"Most belly dancers never get as good as her," Farida said.

The belly dancing segment ended, and the Moroccan band was replaced by an elderly Spaniard with a guitar, accompanied by a young man. Farida used her lips to toy with her friend's mouth. Her kisses were sadistic, starting softly, then ending suddenly with a bite.

"Do you speak English?" Jerry inquired in English.

"Yes, ma'am," I replied, also in English.

"He's a friend," Rubio interjected. "We always meet at the Petit Socco and sit in Central Café."

"Rubio's a good man," I ventured to say.

"That's why I consider him like my son," the woman agreed.

She extended her veined hands and ran her fingers through his red hair. She gave him the cigarettes.

A thought went through my mind: he's her spoiled child.

"To kick things off," the Spanish singer said into the microphone, "we'll sing for you 'Elborom Bom Biro.'"

He started strumming chords on his guitar, then the boy started to sing, stamping his feet to the tune's rhythm. He looked like a nineteenth-century dancer in Madrid. Extending his arms, he sang about his love, his pride, and his youth.

Love no longer amazes me, I thought.

"Olé! Niño!" Farida cried.

The young singer threw her a grateful look.

"Olé! My boy!" Jerry joined in.

His heels tapped rapidly. His head drooped, then he raised it abruptly. He spread his arms and lifted his head higher, grateful for the enthusiastic audience response.

"And now, we will perform the 'Gypsy Fandango,'" he announced, clearing his throat as he moved his hands over his mouth.

"Viva tu madre!" the audience shouted.

I thought of Spanish delights: Gypsies in Granada, the bull's dance, the rhythmic whispers of the tambourine at night, and bats colliding in the moonlight. Córdoban nights, and a stray boy in love, flirting with his girlfriend by the window of her apartment. *My beloved Gypsy girl, such a good heart! If she steals a piece of bread, she gives me half.* El Fandango Andaluz and a dancer atop a table. A dress spreading like wings in the air, while watching eyes try to steal a lustful look beneath. A street choir singing in the streets and alleys of Barcelona. A farewell song performed on a porch. A caravan of Sevillian girls on a pilgrimage to El Rocío. The melancholic songs of Asturia, and a rhythm played using a key on a pot. Holy Saturday night in Catalonia: *She carries a child. She bears the child in her arms. Jesus calls to her . . .* The shepherds singing in front of the caves. The blind singing their odes on the streets of Madrid. The rugged faces of men in Santiago. The guitar, the oil lamp, a sorrowful song, and bottles of alcohol. La Danza Prima. Danza Pericote. Córdoba Serenata. El Bolero. Charos Salamantinos. El Fandango Andaluz. La Danza Mona in Galicia. Arisco de Vizcaya. La Jota in Aragón. La Sardana. La Farandola in Andorra. *On a dune of sand, I will sweep you, little girl. On a dune of sand, I will sweep you. The girl responds with a thrust of her head, the toe of her foot.* El

Jaleo in the bars of Sevilla. La Danza Paranda in Murcia. The dance of San Antonio de la Flórida. The festival of the Cathedral of Corpus Christi. Acrobacias de Valls in the streets of Barcelona. The dance of swords in Pontevedra. The dance of dwarves and giants in Alicante. Moroccan parties of Muslims in Alcoy. The dance of bows in San Sebastián. The ribbon dance in Huesca and Tenerife. Dancing all over, as wine removes the veil of shyness and awakens love.

"Farida!" shouted a drunken woman who had just entered. "My dear Farida!"

They embraced.

"Alia! Alia, my dear!" Farida responded, a bit drunk herself.

"It's so good to see you, Farida!"

The audience's applause for the male singer overwhelmed their words. The young man bowed several times with a feminine flexibility, then left the stage with a rhythmic flair.

Tango music started playing. Rubio took Jerry's veined hand and pulled her to the dance floor. Farida's friend accepted her drunken, sleepy kisses. Farida turned to me, smiling.

"So, do you know the Soho and Piccadilly neighborhoods well?" I asked her.

"Have you been there?" she asked, eyes sparkling.

"No. I just asked that so I don't fall asleep again."

"You're right," she replied with a laugh. "We should say or do something so we don't fall asleep. I hate sleeping."

She went on, "I worked at the Omar Khayyam disco in London."

She poured me a drink and looked at Jerry, who was behaving like an infatuated teenager with Rubio. Nearby, two women gazed at each other, smiling.

The world's a wild dance featuring a man and woman, I thought, and then two women smiling at each other.

A drunk young man stopped in front of Farida.

"Let's dance!" he said. "Come on."

He stretched out his hand and grabbed her wrist.

Farida's friend's face twisted in anger.

"You know who I am," the boy added.

"Yes, I know who you are. I'll dance with you, but enough of this selfishness, Karim."

She got up to dance with the young man. Farida's friend stood up and left.

A man came home in the morning from his night shift and found his wife sleeping in his bed with another man. He quietly stole to the kitchen and prepared breakfast for them. His wife left with her lover and never came back.

Nora took to the dance floor with some guy. I love tango. It carries a delicious sense of nostalgia. I thought about Nora.

I love her as much as I want her to love me, I told myself.

Farida came back, followed by the young fellow who'd asked her to dance.

"Where did he go?" she asked, her voice panicked.

"He left," I said.

She walked toward the exit and spoke with the waiter. She returned and collapsed on the couch. "Oof! I'm so tired of jealous men."

The young guy came up to her.

"Come on, Farida!" he said. "You've forgotten about me."

She extended her hand to her glass and banged it on the table. I imagined a sailor crushing a paper cup after finishing his drink.

"What do you want from her?" Alia said to the guy. "Leave her alone now."

One of the guests interceded and took the drunk guy back toward the bar. He returned with a fresh empty glass and cleaned the table.

"It's all fine now," he said.

Jerry returned with Rubio, overflowing with happiness. She gave us a look.

"What happened here?" she asked.

I thought of a dead tree in the rain.

"Farida's friend left," I told her in English. "A glass got broken. And someone Farida used to know is pestering her to dance with him."

"Some old friendships cause us a lot of trouble," Jerry said.

Farida poured whiskey and water into her glass, her nerves frayed. It was five in the morning. I was still sober.

Rubio nagged Jerry to leave.

"Listen, Rubio," Farida said sharply. "Leave the woman alone and have a drink if you want. You're sitting with a woman who possesses this."

She raised her hand and rubbed thumb and forefinger together. Then she picked up a bundle of banknotes and turned to me.

"I lost a million and a half francs this month in a completely annoying way," she said. "Even so, I don't know how to rid myself of such bad habits."

I took a sip from my glass.

She's right, I thought. Like the others, I too drink from her generosity with no right. The only thing good about me is that I don't bother her in any way, and try to agree with everything she says. She is seeking a harmony of time, place, and people, the existential trio—something that fascinates me too, though all my attempts to find such a harmony have ended in failure.

The last disco guests were leaving. Although Farida was drunk, she was holding up well. Jerry whispered some Italian words in Rubio's ear.

"*Niente! Niente!*" he yelled, like a spoiled, stubborn brat.

Standing up, he went away, waiting for Jerry to follow him.

"That's what happens when you stay up late with children," Farida said.

"Sometimes he's simply unbearable," Jerry said in English.

"People like him live and die without ever maturing," Farida said. "They are truly unbearable."

"Do you want me," Jerry asked after a pause, "to come over and sleep at your place?"

"Me? No, sweetie. I don't want to sleep."

Jerry got up and kissed Farida, then took Rubio's arm and left.

"How depressing to think I might end up with a blond boy when I get to be as old as her," Farida said. "He's her grandchildren's age, and yet she treats him like a lover."

As for me, I thought, when I grow old, I'll start loving and desiring women without feeling miserable. I won't feel any lust to hinder love, or passion to spoil lust. Everything will go just as it comes. I won't lose myself in other people's banalities. Relationships with others are mere delusions. Nostalgia for my old recklessness stops my emotions maturing. Men are bulls and women are cows. I'm a bull to-night, and Nora's the cow that's refusing to let me smell her. Mmmm . . . !

Farida stared at me.

"You don't seem to care about any of this," she said. "What are you thinking about?"

"I'm thinking about a human cow." I paused and laughed.

"Where's your friend Nora?" she asked. "I think she left," she added with a laugh. "And that human bull followed her."

"You're on a break, then," I said after a moment.

"No, I'm not on a break," she replied, her lips parted in a sneer. "I'm a stupid woman. Before I traveled to London, a man I used to love told me, 'One day, when I want it, you'll return to me.' I scoffed, but here I am back for him."

"He's my father's age," she went on after a pause. "I thought my father had died. He left me when I was a kid and divorced my mother. When I arrived back in Tangier, though, I was told that he was still alive, in Casablanca. That was shocking news for me; I felt upset and happy at the same time. The strange thing is that as soon as I knew my father was still alive, I started to hate the man I came back for."

She stood up.

"Aren't you going to leave?" she asked.

I left with her, without asking where she was going. The morning's sweetness greeted me.

"Where are you headed?" I finally asked her.

She looked at me, licking her lips nervously. "I'm going for a swim in the sea. After that I'll go to the hotel to sleep. I'm staying in the Hotel Marina, if you want to visit."

I liked her and didn't like her. Before she disappeared, she gave me a wave.

Samir came over. "Let's go to Café Pilo," he said.

"Okay."

This café-nightclub was of the hour, its doors open to welcome everyone that bars spit out at the end of the night. I do not like looking at people's faces in the morning, whether the ones who have slept or those who haven't gone to sleep yet. Their faces always look worried.

"You don't know Farida yet," Samir said. "She likes old men because in each old man she can see the father she lost."

Near Café Negresco, we saw a girl standing idly.

"Do you know her?" Samir asked.

"No."

"I know her. Take her with you if you want. She won't mind. I'll introduce you. She isn't a professional yet."

She looked to be about sixteen. We moved toward her. Her clothes were tidy. She didn't look as if she'd spent the night drinking. She and Samir shook hands, then he introduced her to me.

"Zahra."

"Idris."

I felt her warm hand in mine.

"I'm hungry," Samir said. "I'm going to go to the barbecue vendor at Café Atlas."

"Leave me with Miss Zahra for a bit," I told him.

He laughed and left. I thought about the Hotel Marina. Farida was about to float in the sea. I too was about to float.

Tangier, 1967

The Impossible

In existence, there is an immense gap we pass through, bit by bit, until we reach an abyss of total nothingness.

That was what Ismael told her. Señora Mary pitied Ismael when he was sad, and pitied most of the rest of her three sons' friends as well.

"Don't worry. When your financial situation improves, you'll stop feeling sorry for yourself."

Ismael was respectful when she spoke, but he did not really care what she said. He only liked her because she listened to his complaints about life and his bad luck in this city, something that had started to irritate him.

"Maybe, but I might be worried about some other aspiration than money. I might never be lucky at anything, whether here or anywhere else."

"I believe that luck will knock on your door. People who suffer at the beginning of their lives often end up leading happy ones."

He did not want to argue with her. Why should he care about the end of his life, even if it were full of happiness?

"What my mother says is true," Nael said. "Everything depends on money. My mother always knows what she's talking about."

Señora Mary looked at her eldest son with pleasure. Nael did not like his mother talking with the likes of Ismael, consoling him in his agony. He felt that some of her happiness was stolen from him and given to others. He had once had an uncomfortable word with her while she was talking to one of Rafiq's friends.

"Mama," he had said, "please lower your voice a little. Everyone in the coffee shop can hear you."

Ismael thought about Nael: There he is now, sitting peacefully, head leaning forward, forehead slanted back. His hair is light like a young bird's feathers, his cheeks are rosy, his skin light as though polished with varnish, his glasses thick. A few days ago, he celebrated his twenty-fifth birthday.

Jean entered and greeted them. He shook Señora Mary's hand and sat down next to her, while Nael looked angrily in his direction.

"How are you today, Señora?" Jean asked in his sheep-like voice.

"I'm okay. Everything is as God wills it. And you, my son," she asked in French, warped by her Spanish accent, "are you well?"

"I'm fine, thank you."

"Your health's good?"

"It's fine, thank you."

"Thank God. If your health's good, then everything's all right."

"The weather's nice today."

"Indeed it is. I hope it stays that way for the next few days."

Nael rubbed his forehead with his fingers, then stood up frowning. He smoothed his clothes, put his hands in his trouser pockets, puffed out his chest, and shook himself, stretching his feet out front, then back.

"Mama, let's go. It's lunchtime."

She looked at him silently. She was not quite ready to go. Ismael and Jean stood up and said good-bye.

She was around forty-five years old, but anyone looking at her from behind while she was walking or standing, or from a distance, would think she was a young woman.

Fadila came in, sat down, stretched, and sighed. She did not conceal her morning paleness behind any kind of psychedelic makeup. She took out a box of her yellow cigarettes and lit one with a gold lighter. Taking a deep drag, she blew the smoke energetically toward the ceiling. She took another puff; this time she blew the smoke out in small *O*'s.

"What are you dreaming about?" she asked Ismael.

"Nothing."

"Don't sit there silent. Say something."

He didn't want to tell her anything. He craved the smell of her body, something that she used to leave in his bed when she slept in it with Rafiq's female friend. It tempted him to take her by force, but he swallowed his lust and made do with making her feel embarrassed.

He remembered the day when he'd come to the house and found her waiting for Rafiq.

"Fadila," he'd said, his strong voice surprising her.

"Yes?" she replied, somewhat taken aback.

"You're fabulous."

"Really?" she said, smiling widely. She went on, "You only find me fabulous when you're drunk."

Maybe I've come to hate women, he thought. He focused his attention on a knife lying on top of a pile of books covered in dust and neglect. Maybe I will kill a beautiful woman of her type, and that'll be that. The attitude of women like her annoys me.

"Ismael, why are you looking at things like that? Has something happened to you?"

"Oh, no," he said. "Are you scared of me?"

"Me? No. What are you saying, Ismael? I just don't like seeing you so distracted. I always like to have a good time with you."

She sat down on the bed, leaning on her elbows, staring at him and moving her legs, trying to smile. To hide her nervousness, she got up and came over to him.

"Rafiq's later than usual today."

"If he doesn't come, I'm definitely going to have a word with him."

He leaned on the sofa and lit a cigarette. He heard her body bump into the bathroom door.

"Ismael! Ismael!" she yelled. "It's still there!"

She reentered the room and ran over to the bed, frightened.

"It's still there!" she yelled.

"What's there?"

"The mouse. You didn't kill it. Why did you lie to me?"

"It's another mouse. I saw it, but I couldn't get it."

"You lie. You didn't kill it. You're sorry for those dirty animals."

"Are you stupid or what? Why would I feel sorry for those animals when they destroy my books?"

He went over to the stack of books in the corner and showed her books and journals with their edges eaten away.

"I don't believe you," she said, lying down at the edge of the bed. "You love those creatures. Rafiq found a piece of bread soaked in oil in the kitchen near the opening where the mice live."

"That's crazy."

"I don't believe you. You're raising those animals. Rafiq doesn't lie. He saw you here playing with a cockroach and a frog. You were trying to leap like it and copying its croak."

"You two are both crazy. Enough of this absurdity."

"I won't come here anymore."

Ismael did a dance in his imagination. That's what I want, Ismael told himself, That's what I devoutly desire! You're the one who threw some of my journals in the toilet . . .

Rafiq had started getting tired of his job supervising workers in the coffee shop–restaurant that the family owned. It did not take long for him to become friends with the waiters. He usually took his meals in the kitchen, listening to the old Moroccan chef telling him about life in Tangier thirty or forty years ago.

"Waiters are used to obeying orders," his father, Sayyid Abed al-Baqi, had told him. "You must realize that we lose our standing if we show them any sympathy. It makes them lazy, and they do what they want. Have your meals in the restaurant, not in the kitchen. Be firm with them and use as few words as possible, so they'll respect you."

Rafiq worshipped his father, just as Nael worshipped their mother. He knew that his father was stubborn and that it was impossible to change his opinions. To avoid any deterioration in his relationship with his father, he'd quit his job.

Rafiq, Fadila, and Ismael all went down from the new city to explore life in the historic quarter, as they used to do once or twice a month. Fadila wore a pink blouse, glossy and transparent, which fit tightly to her body. She styled her hair like Cleopatra, used the most expensive makeup on her face, and sprayed herself with high-class French perfume. Rafiq wore a simple shirt and pants, as always when he went for a stroll in the old town.

Entering the flea market, they found the auction had just begun. Here and there brokers yelled the prices of old and new goods. Every time they passed a stall with old clothes, Rafiq stopped. He'd grab a shirt, pants, or shoes, examine them briefly with feigned interest, and talk about the history of the garment, or of that shoe and its type. Then he would apologize to the vendor and continue the tour.

"I don't know why Rafiq comes here to touch these used items without ever buying anything," a bored Fadila said.

"That's my business," Rafiq responded, "so shut up!"

At one of the three exits from the market, Rafiq suggested that they go into a restaurant for some bessara.

"I haven't eaten it in months. It's good here. Do you remember that morning we had it here?"

"Yes, I do," Ismael replied. "It was around six a.m. We left the Monocle bar and came here."

"I won't have any," Fadila said. "I'm not going inside."

"Eat it or not, you're coming in with us," Rafiq answered her sharply. "Do you hear me?"

Her face paled; she lowered her head and went in behind them. In the small, dark, dirty room they found five men eating bessara. The men looked at them curiously. Fadila busied herself choosing a place to sit on one of the long, low, dirty benches. Ismael sat down, and Rafiq beckoned Fadila to sit next to him. They ordered two bowls of bessara with olive oil, harissa, and whole-wheat bread. Plastic pitchers stood on each of the three tables. The waiter gave them bowls and filled a pitcher of water for them, all the while casting curious glances their way, just as the five men were doing. One of them gave Fadila a scornful look mixed with lust. Fadila focused her gaze on the ceiling or at the boy doing the dishes in the sink. The boy bowed his head and looked away toward the kitchen.

One of the men finished eating.

"What about those people?" he asked the restaurant's owner while paying for his meal. "Are they Muslims?"

"God knows."

Ismael and Rafiq ate and drank happily, while Fadila continued to stare at the ceiling, the boy, and the void.

Upon leaving, Fadila took a deep breath and quickly lit a cigarette. She turned around as if she'd forgotten something.

"Did I get dirty?" she asked Ismael.

He looked at her small flat butt as if seeing it for the first time.

"I don't see anything," he said.

She put her cigarette in her mouth and her purse in her left hand. With her right hand she brushed off her butt, as if something actually was stuck to her clothes.

They took a cab from the outdoor souk to Hafa Café. They sat on the terrace overlooking the sea. Rafiq took a deep drag from his hash-filled cigarette.

"In the beginning," Rafiq said, "there was nothing in the world but sky and sea."

"What about before sky and sea?" Fadila countered.

"Don't go too far. Sky and sea are enough."

A half dozen Moroccans were sitting on a mat under a small tree, smoking hash and joking while a musician played traditional melodies on the mandolin.

"And you," Rafiq said, looking at Ismael, "what do you think about this, my dear?"

"You're right. It's enough to know that the world started from water, that life sprang from water."

One of the groups nearby started singing, accompanied by the mandolin:

My soul, what betrayal.

You've made me lose myself.

My days pass by, a loss.

For what, all my suffering?

That evening in the café, Fadila looked very delicate as she sat there, contentedly smoking her hash-filled cigarette. Ismael gave her a playful push. She choked and coughed, then lit another cigarette.

"Touch is the most delicate sense," Ismael told her. "I can never be sure something really exists until I touch it. Other senses can be deceptive."

He gave her a gentle touch.

"Look," he said, "you're more present like this than you would be without my touch."

"Ismael, please don't touch me like that again," she said lightly.

Goosebumps rose all over her body as she felt his gentle

touch. As Rafiq looked beyond the sea to the horizon, Fadila drew inward as Ismael caressed her.

Habiba had come from Rabat, running away from her family. She quit her job in nursing because she could not live apart from Nael.

Ismael and Rafiq were sitting in Coleridge Café, drinking.

"My father can't imagine Nael and Habiba getting married," Rafiq commented. "Do you mind if she stays with you?" he went on. "We're going to try to convince Nael to break up with her. He can visit her at your place, but my father will make him come home by eleven p.m."

Ismael could not refuse to take in Habiba, nor could he deny her the bed. Drinking Spanish wine, Ismael was lying down opposite her on the Moroccan sofa where he used to sleep. It was raining hard, and the wind was blowing. Habiba was lying on the bed. The fire crackled every time he put another log on. Rain, wind, thunder, and silence, occasionally interrupted by a noisy barking dog or a frog croaking nearby.

"Are you going to sleep now?" he asked her as she fidgeted in bed.

"Yes."

She lay on her right side facing him. A neighbor's window on the top floor clanked shut. The rain was coming down hard. She changed position, then sat up.

"What was that?" she asked.

"Nothing."

"This storm won't let me sleep."

"Are you scared?"

She looked at him, shaking her head. "No, what should I be scared of?"

"Maybe you're afraid of something."

"I'm not used to sleeping in this room yet."

He filled his glass.

"Would you like a glass?"

"No, thank you."

He paused. "You don't drink?"

"I drink a little sometimes."

"Have a glass then. Maybe it'll help you relax and sleep."

"Thank you, but I don't want any right now. Have you got a novel I can read?"

He got up, looked over his books, and handed her *The Stranger*. "Have you read this?"

"No."

"I think you'll like it."

He sat on the sofa and watched the shadow of the lamp on the ceiling.

"Meursault's a strange person, preoccupied but worthy of pity," he said. "That's what Nicolette told me when she read the novel. Do you think there's anyone who really complicates his life in that way, in a society that doesn't demand such complications? I think Camus is emptying all the agony of life that he experienced during his miserable days in Algeria into his hero's head."

"Maybe so," Habiba replied. "He devoted his entire life to a serious and compassionate examination of human existence and its fate. But what about you? Aren't you reading anything now?"

"I'm drinking, and I can't think clearly when I drink. I'm a bit worried too."

"Why?"

"I don't know."

"Because I'm staying with you here?"

"No. It's something personal."

He paused for a moment. "Do you like the way the novel begins?" he asked.

"Yes, the style's simple."

"Aren't you going to work today?" she asked him the following morning.

"I don't work today." He looked at his broken watch. "What time is it?" he asked her.

"A few minutes past nine. My watch isn't very accurate. It could be nine."

"When is Nael coming?"

"He doesn't wake up before ten."

He put on his coat.

"Won't you stay until Nael comes," she asked, "so we can have breakfast together here?"

"No, thanks. I'll just go to Esquima Café."

When he returned in the evening, he found Señora Mary and Habiba having black tea with lemon, accompanied by sweets from a gold-paper container. He noticed a certain mute tension in Habiba's expression.

Señora Mary has always stood by Habiba, he told himself.

"I never imagined that you owned so many books," Mary said.

"You can see."

"Do you find time to read them all?"

"No, it's impossible."

"So, why do you buy more books than you can read?"

"Because I'm totally obsessed with buying books."

She shook her head, smiling.

"I see," she said. "You've a wonderful hobby to entertain yourself. A book is the best of friends. But you shouldn't spend too long reading difficult books lest you ruin your health. People who spend a lot of time reading hard books don't end up well."

He smiled at her. In his imagination he let out a crazy laugh.

After she'd left, Habiba exploded with anger over Nael's family.

"They're like rotten sardines!" she said.

"That's true."

"I gave up everything for Nael. For four years now, his family has known full well about my relationship with him. Do they think I'm going to keep on making him happy while they find him a girl from a rich family like theirs?"

"That's the way such people think. How did Nael behave with you this evening?"

"As usual," she said, nervously lighting a cigarette. "He stayed until ten. He can't change anything. I've started to hate him. He's just a big baby!"

Ismael poured himself a glass. She asked him to pour one for her too. She looked at him fondly as he handed her the drink. He glanced at *The Stranger* next to her and sat on the edge of the bed.

"Do you like the book?" he asked.

She picked it up.

"Ahh . . . ," she said, "I'm troubled by the hero's conduct.

He's very unlucky. I don't think he's harsh, but he's stubborn. I think that he likes other people more than himself."

"Could you live with a man like him?" he asked jokingly.

"I don't know," she replied. "That's a different story."

Their eyes met, and they smiled at each other.

"I'm an idiot."

"Why?"

"It doesn't matter. I'm just an idiot, and that's enough."

"It's the circumstances."

"I'm more optimistic than I should be. Everything that happens to me seems normal at first, then something unexpected happens."

He poured two more glasses.

"You have beautiful hands."

"Just hands."

"Has he ever promised marriage before?"

"Of course. Why else would I stay with him for four years?"

Later that evening, Ismael found Rafiq and Fadila at Zaggora Café, drinking and laughing like children. He sat down with them and ordered a glass of wine.

"Nael's gone to London," Rafiq told him. "That's what my dad decided."

"What about Habiba?"

"She can do whatever she wants. He's going to stay there for around six months to learn English. My father thinks that when he comes back, he'll hire him to be our hotel's accountant."

"She's miserable and alone. When she finds out that he's gone abroad, she might have a nervous breakdown."

"She can follow him there if she wants."

"She's filthy," Fadila interjected.

"How so?" Ismael asked.

"She says nasty things about Rafiq's family, and about me as well. Last year, when I fought with Rafiq and went away to Paris, she told a friend from Rabat whom I know well that I went there to be a whore. Do you think that's reasonable?"

"I don't know anything about it. With me she only talks about her bad luck."

"And what else does she tell you about herself?" she asked, her voice cynical. "Tell me the truth, Ismael."

"She says that she's miserable and regrets quitting her job for Nael."

"Is that all, Ismael? She's lying. That isn't the full story. My friend from Rabat told me all about her; she knows her well. She wants to become someone important on the back of Nael's family."

"Her mother works as a laundry woman in people's houses," she went on scornfully, "her father's an unemployed alcoholic, and her brother's a wretch."

"And that's her fault?"

"She lied to Nael when he asked her about her family."

"I see. Now I understand."

"It's better for her to go back to Rabat and look for a life that suits her."

"My mother will visit her tomorrow," Rafiq said. "She'll give her some money to go back to Rabat."

"Nael never loved her," Fadila said. "She knows that, but she still stalks him everywhere he goes."

"Why do you care about her so much?" Rafiq asked Ismael.

"Because she's miserable."

"Save her if you can," Fadila said sarcastically.

"She might be a good girlfriend for someone who suits her," Rafiq added.

Ismael realized that they were making fun of him.

"That's nothing to do with me. I'm not the one who promised her marriage; that was Nael."

"She's lying," Rafiq said. "Nael told my mother everything. He would never lie to my mother—you know that."

"I know." Ismael smiled wryly.

"She's had two abortions," Rafiq said. "That pregnancy game doesn't work anymore."

"Did you kill that mouse yet?" Fadila asked.

"Habiba killed it, but now another one's appeared. It's the worst mouse I've ever seen. It's not scared of anything. It's stupid. The old one was much smarter than this new stubborn, ferocious one."

"Really?" she asked in disbelief. "Habiba killed it herself? That can't be true."

"What's so strange about that? It's just a little mouse."

"Ahh . . . ," she said in disbelief. "Maybe. She must be used to killing mice."

"She even saw some cockroaches," Ismael scoffed, "and she wasn't scared of them either."

Fadila's whole body shivered with disgust.

"She's used to everything," she went on. "You need to start looking for a place on a higher floor, Ismael. Ground-floor apartments are always infested with these dirty creatures and bugs. Unless, of course, you like them."

Seeing the disgusted look Ismael was giving her, she looked at her watch.

"Oh Rafiq," she said, "we're late! Jean is waiting for us."

Rafiq invited Ismael to join them.

"I can't stand his manner," Ismael said.

"He's bought a new kind of hash."

"That's right," Fadila said. "Today Jean's bought an expensive type. He's also redecorated his apartment with fancy new furniture."

"You can come with us if you want," Rafiq said.

Tangier, January 1967

The Spiderweb

"I'm a shoemaker, a shoemaker from Larache. Who remembers me today in Tangier?"

He had been shouting for a while.

Tottering, he looked this way and that. He laughed, he tottered. Putting his hand in the pockets of his pants, he took out some torn shreds.

"All I have is holes," he yelled. "Holes! Holes!"

Most of the guests in the coffeehouses overlooking the square were watching him, annoyed and suspicious. He went and stood in the center of the square, smiling and laughing. He kept winking at passersby, men and women. He was still tottering as he thought about himself. An empty tin box dropped in front of him.

"My turn," he said to a kid.

He kicked it toward the kid, and the two kicked it back and forth.

"Take your can and scram," a man yelled to the kid.

A young man spat in Alal's face. Cursing him, Alal wiped the spit off with his jacket sleeve. The young man spat in his face again. Alal winked at him, waving his arms in the air in a circle. He went onto the terrace of Café Tanjis. A foreigner offered him a cigarette. The man also let him drink the rest of his bottle of orangeade.

The young man went over to him.

"Get out of here!" he yelled. "Why are you drinking in the month of Ramadan?"

Alal laughed. The young man punched him hard in the face. Alal fell against the iron railing encircling the terrace. His body sagged as his head hit the ground. Streams of blood exploded from his head.

"Well done!" someone else told the young man. "He deserves that and more."

Similar pronouncements could be heard from most of the café customers.

"Son of a bitch," the young man said proudly as he walked slowly away. "One never knows how the likes of him end up in this happy city."

"Hey you, wait! Can't you see he's bleeding?"

"Dog! He doesn't even respect the holy month!" the young man said aggressively. "I'll call an ambulance."

A crowd of customers and bystanders gathered around him.

"Wait until the police arrive."

"He's dying."

"You're right. He's dying."

"He's slipping away."

"He's dead."

"Right. He's dead."

"Poor man! This is God's will."

"Call the police quickly."

The young man was unable to escape the growing crowd as it circled around him.

"You all saw that I didn't kill him."

"But no one told you to hit him like that."

He heard the voice of a Café Tanjis waiter: "People like him just don't get up when they fall."

A man closed Alal's eyelids and covered his face with a handkerchief. It was soon soaked in blood, a red mask. The kid appeared again with the tin box in his hand.

"Go home," a man yelled at him.

"I didn't mean to kill him," the young man screamed tearfully.

Crazy Carly appeared in the square. He turned toward the crowd, giggling loudly, a marijuana joint quivering in his hand. The police arrived in the square.

"I didn't kill him . . . I didn't kill him . . . "

Carly giggled crazily. The young man collapsed into the hands of the police. Carly looked up at the sky and burst into raucous laughter.

Tangier, 1968

Night and Sea

She had the overwhelming sense that the beach was hers alone. In the distance, an old Hindu with a limp was throwing pieces of bread for the seabirds. She stopped and looked at the small beach houses. Most of the doors had been removed. All the bars were closed. The short Hindu started walking away, leaving the chilly beach, tossing the remaining breadcrumbs into the air, followed by a small swarm of birds. His bald head swayed from side to side, matching his limp. While the birds kept chasing after him, Widad yanked off her shoes and dropped them on the sand beside her bag. It started raining, a warm rain. Her hair was soaked as she let the waves lick her feet. Eyes closed, she lifted her face. The raindrops fell into her half-open mouth, a pleasure she was used to savoring in the shower. She picked up her shoes and bag and started walking barefoot, gazing at her footprints in the sand. Her sad feelings intensified, yet no single emotion arose that she could clearly identify.

Passing by a shapeless pond on the long walkway by the beach, she entered the Atlas bar and asked for a Bloody Mary. She went into the bathroom to dry her wet hair. At the end of the bar, a young man was sitting with a young woman who was silently sobbing. He talked to her in an aggravated tone as he smoked and sipped at this drink. He swore to her that Nadia was just a work colleague.

"What's with the heavy rain these days?" said a foreigner to his friend, the owner of the English bar.

"It's the year for floods in Morocco," the bar owner replied.

Widad sat on the sofa and followed their conversation without catching a word of what they were saying. She smiled as her eyes met the foreigner's.

The young man put the change in his pocket. His girl had stopped crying. He joked with her, patted her hair and face, then held her hand in his. A song started playing: "Oh God! I'm the sinner! But her, but her, never let her suffer . . . "

The door crashed open and Zoubida came in, drunk. She had the eyes of a cow. She was tall, and her body was ready to please a line of victorious soldiers returning from war. She greeted Widad. The waiter poured her a glass of wine and placed a small pot near her. She filled a spoon from the pot and stirred it in the wine.

Nabil also sometimes adds salt to his beer, Widad thought, so he doesn't get drunk too quickly.

"For the last three days," Zoubida told Widad. "I haven't slept more than two or three hours a night."

She took off her shoes and stood there barefoot.

"This will soothe my stomach. I can feel my head boiling."

Widad felt as though her desire to talk was wedged inside her throat. She was thinking of all those men with whom she was sleeping without any dreams for the future.

She gazed at the sea. The sky was cloudy; it was getting dark, and the pouring rain was slapping at the windows. The bar owner and his friend were chatting. A fragrant flower was growing in Widad's melancholic thoughts. Her craving for all the things that she loved but could never acquire pained her. She could not stand having an empty glass, and waved for the bartender to refill it. Lightning, followed by powerful thunder. Zoubida shivered. She exchanged a mysterious look with Widad. The sea and sky were storming.

"I can't stand thunder," Zoubida said.

Suddenly a white cat appeared in the hall. It meowed at Zoubida, begging for something. Zoubida looked at it, startled.

"Is the cat friendly?" she asked Widad.

Widad was surprised. "It's just a cat," she replied.

"Cats are never just cats. Once my mother was preparing some fish, and there was a cat meowing innocently near her. When she tried to shoo it away, the cat attacked her and stuck its teeth and claws into her arms. Two days later, the same cat returned to the house. My mother had every reason to punish it and locked it up in a small room. A few days later, we opened the door. The cat was just a ghost, barely moving, unable to walk. Its gaze was crazy; it looked really scary.

"'We should give it some food and water,' I told my mother.

"'Never! I'd rather it die from starvation,' she yelled. 'It's possessed by the devil. We ought to kill the devil in it. Take it somewhere far away, where it can't find anything to eat.'

"My little brother Mustafa and I put it in a basket and took it far away to a deserted area. I asked my brother to stay by the cat and wait until I returned. He asked me why, and I said I wanted to try to find some food and water for the cat so that it might stay alive.

"'I'll tell Mother,' he said.

"We left it there and returned home. Mustafa was jumping around and kicking empty cans with his feet. I was feeling sorry for the cat, which was going to die of starvation. That night, my mother was choked by the cat's ghost. The following morning, we took some food and water and went looking for the cat, hoping to save it if it was still alive. We couldn't find it. I tried to persuade my mother that someone else might have found the cat and saved it.

"'No way. Its dead soul was the ghost that spent last night strangling me.'

"My mother lived for years after that incident, but she was never able to rid herself of the cat's ghost before she died."

"Is that why you're always so keen to exert your mother's revenge on cats whenever they appear?"

"Me? Never. But I'm not fond of them."

Zoubida asked the bartender to refill their glasses. Widad thought of Miloud's Persian cat. Miloud was single, and he used to feed his beautiful cat from his plate. He bathed it himself, and it slept on his bed. When it got old and sick and its beautiful fur started to fall out, he filled the bathtub with water. Clasping the cat by its back, he held it under until it drowned.

The loudspeaker was playing the song "I was twenty years old when I used to waste time on stupid things."

He took out his notepad and wrote, "Hope is coincidence, assumption is good faith. How many times have I hugged a man I hated, and all for the sake of a reckless woman, because the two of us shared her love."

He gave Widad a passionate look.

"What are you writing?" she asked him.

"Thoughts . . . "

"People's night, my naked night. Cruel, deserted night. Two beetles fighting over a dead mouse. Magian night; they used to love depressing nights."

He was sitting near the window, contemplating the stars and writing, while Widad, in her nightgown, was lying across the bed, her feet on the ground.

Suddenly he felt bored.

"People suffer pain because God doesn't," he wrote. "He never gets sad, because he knows everything. But we human beings suffer a lot, in order to know just a little."

He no longer knew how to sift his own thoughts. He took a sip from his glass. With him, Widad had the feeling that she was an orphan. He had a career path. He would finish his degree and become a professor of philosophy. He would find another woman. I will keep sleeping with men I don't love.

She thought about throwing him out; never again would he be in her apartment. But her heart skipped a beat. Changing her mind, she gave him a loving look, deeply immersed as he was in writing down ideas that he did not understand.

Nabil was sitting on the sand, his hands clasped around his knees, while Widad performed her relaxation ritual, walking along the shore and letting the waves lap over her feet.

She came back refreshed. He was writing his thoughts in his notebook.

She is like a stemless flower, he thought.

"Forest night is better than beach night," he wrote. "I like the sounds: owls, bats, crickets, frogs, foxes. But here, everything's buried in sand."

To them the sea looked divided against itself, the green color close in, the blue farther out. The sea horizon formed a field of white flowers coated with fog.

As he picked up a handful of sand, his eyes met hers with glowing desire. He closed his eyes and felt her warm breath on his face. His hand let the sand fall. They embraced. Bare skin always tempted him with the warmth of her body.

She looked at the faces lining the bar. A young man was sitting by himself, drinking and talking to a flower, while he consulted the mirror in front of him to acknowledge their conversation. Widad felt herself desired by all the men. Samir was looking at her, showing off his jacket. She pictured them as a group of maniacs, taking turns to rape her. The bar was packed with men, and five or six escort girls were entertaining more than one guest at a time. Each was drinking a glass with one man, while other glasses awaited them elsewhere. Widad hated herself when she felt so desired. She was afraid that someone other than Nabil would fall in love with her. She believed that even lust contained a little love. Her usual customer paid her well. He was old and married and treated her kindly. But he wasn't there tonight.

"I can only understand Widad when she's far away from me," Nabil wrote in his notebook. "My life gets connected through this sense of distance, which shapes its attributes. Even with music, I can only enjoy it when it reaches me as distant waves. The scenery is more inspiring when I can get far enough away to see the abyss. Dizziness overwhelms me and cleanses my mind of obsessive thoughts, like people who have electroshock therapy at mental asylums. My true self stands apart, on the opposite shore from a lighthouse, revealed with its crazy lamp. I am tired of people who are clever by themselves and crazy with other people."

She was still by herself when a black Moroccan entered. He was handsome and elegant. He sat at a table with two others and began to describe how he had saved a young woman at the beach from drowning.

"I hate ungrateful people," he said suddenly in a loud voice.

Widad could not stop looking at him. He winked at her with his right eye, and his tongue appeared in his half-open mouth.

"He's got me," she told herself. "I should not have looked at him. I've never slept with a black man before."

A little girl entered with her arm held out in front of her. Widad asked her to come over and took hold of her outstretched hand.

"What's your name?"

"Rahma."

"Where's your mother?"

"She's waiting outside."

She gave her money and gently sent her away.

Widad noticed a hand like a crow resting lightly on her shoulder. She felt the hand slip down her back. So he was the first black person to touch her. She looked at him seductively. He smiled at her. His eyes were delightful. She thought she might not be able to please him in any way. She had that feeling whenever a man desired her, but she did not desire him. A night of profundities.

She stayed quiet. He pressed the tips of his fingers into her back:

"Do you like it?"

She looked at him without saying a word. He seemed like a child who does not deserve to be punished. He kissed her on the cheek. His breath was alcohol-laden and heavy. She imagined herself in the wildest place. She stood up and walked away amid lustful drunken gazes, and the black man followed her.

Tangier, 1968

The Strange Corpse

Screams in the big courtyard. A living body falls to the ground. People rush in, running from everywhere. The dying body looks up at the bright sky. The light in his eyes goes out bit by bit. He is motionless.

Ten o'clock in the morning. People rush in from all directions. The sun awakens in memory, that old god.

"He can't move any longer."

"No one can make him move. He died very strangely. A scary incident."

People at the windows, on balconies and roofs, even in the trees. They arrive, on and on, from every direction, by foot or riding, healthy and sick, old and young, rich and poor. They all realize there's something strange about the corpse. No one can go near it.

Eleven o'clock in the morning. The corpse is still there. Many people sit there watching. Every now and then, some people who have been standing join those sitting. Their eyes never tire of staring at the corpse. Sparks start to fly from the corpse.

They yawn, doze, have iced drinks, eat sandwiches,

smoke, chew gum, smile, flirt, laugh, and push each other, jokingly or seriously, as they try to find a good spot to stand or sit. They drift here and there. They try to understand what is so strange about the corpse. They go for a short stroll and disappear, then they come back again, either by themselves or with newcomers.

Eleven-thirty. Many employees arrive in the courtyard. They're astonished. They have left their offices early to look at the graying corpse as it begins to decompose. The sun is blazing. They use their napkins and sleeves to wipe off their sweat. They jostle to get a spot in the shade of a tree or beneath the awnings of shops and cafés. An old man loses his balance and staggers, collapsing against a girl standing nearby. Women scream. Children burst into tears. The girl looks horrified.

"It's just a dizzy spell. Don't worry. He isn't dead. It looks as though the hot sun has got to him."

"Go home!" (He looks all around him: where does the old man live?) "You can't stay here under the burning sun."

"Leave me alone," the old man says, moving weakly. "Get me some water."

A few minutes past noon. Employees and businessmen are now on their way to the courtyard. Some people standing join those sitting. They're eating their stuffed sandwiches with gusto.

"So, they didn't lie to me. It really is a strange corpse."

"This strange body's been here since ten in the morning."

"Look how it's now emitting that phosphorescent vapor."

"I can see."

"This is the first time I've seen a corpse emit such a vapor."

"It's a strange corpse."

"Are you going to work this afternoon?"

"I don't think so."

"But your bosses are bound to know that you're here, watching to the bitter end as the phosphorus corpse dissolves."

"They're here, too. I don't think they'll go back to work. You'll see."

"A corpse burning up on its own. Who can miss such a spectacle?"

"Indeed, it's a strange phenomenon."

"Maybe it's some new type of human being."

"Possibly."

"Has no one gone near the corpse?"

"Are you crazy? Who would dare? It's burning itself and anyone who goes close to it."

"But nobody has tried so far."

"Who do you think would dare risk his life in such a situation?"

"Weird."

"Why don't you try?"

"Me?"

"Yes."

"Why?"

"To find out if it's still burning or not!"

"You go first."

"I know it's burning."

"How?"

"Look. See how the sparks are flying off it. The strange thing is that there's no smell as there would usually be from a burning corpse."

"It doesn't look like any other corpse."

"Maybe it'll start to smell after sunset."

"I don't think so. The smell from corpses usually spreads more during daytime than at night."

"We'll see."

"Maybe it's a corpse from another world."

"Anything's possible. Who knows?"

They relaxed and enjoyed a nap.

Women and girls now gather in a circle now under one of the sidewalk's trees. One takes off her outer garment, and four of them volunteer to hold it. A second woman takes off her coat, and two others seize its hems. They create shade by raising the dress and coat over the group of kneeling women.

"Poor girl! May it turn out well for her!"

Her baby is crying.

"Don't be afraid, my daughter. Your mother is here with you. She's fine. Don't be afraid. You're with us."

A girl is holding the baby in her arms. She kisses and plays with her. The baby calms down. More and more women gather. They arrive from everywhere to rush into the circle. A little boy approaches and tries to peer into the women's shade. A woman gently pushes him aside:

"Go away. You aren't supposed to see what's happening here."

The boy gives her a stubborn look. "I'm not going," he says grumpily.

She tries pushing him away gently. He scoffs at her and makes her angry.

"Just look at him. He has no shame. Come here once more, and we'll see what happens to you."

They push and shove each other rudely, making the circle even narrower. Poking their noses in here and there, they try to find a spot where they can see what's going on inside the circle. They're arriving from everywhere. The circle grows wider. Some children get lost. Others play hide-and-seek. Screams, tears, laughs. People searching, running, fighting. Waa . . . Waa . . . waaaaaaa . . . !

"A boy! It's a boy!"

"How's the mother doing?"

"Fine."

"She's lucky."

The courtyard is lit more brightly than usual. There are still people arriving from near and far, other towns even. Video cameras film the graying corpse's disintegration. Phosphorescence is still oozing from it. Children fall asleep, hugging their mothers and relatives; others play. Students do their homework, while teachers prepare their lessons or mark their students' work. Presidents and subordinates. The corpse turns to ash. The body parts appear to be scattered. The skull, now separated from the skeleton, shines brighter than the rest of the corpse. People are starting to lose interest in the slowly fading corpse, but they still stay there. They leave for short strolls, then come back to replace the people who have gotten bored just sitting. The people standing and sitting take shifts at the best spots facing the corpse. Many of them are carrying blankets, pillows, cutlery, and gas stoves.

Tangier, October 6, 1971

The Miniature Paradise

Written at the gate of the miniature Paradise:
(I do not think; therefore I am)

"Get out! You can't stay here any longer."
She stared sadly at the guard.
"But why do I have to leave?"
They sip each other's milk and honey.
"The God of Paradise is ordering you out of his Paradise."
They were drinking a kind of alcohol that resembled no
other. No pain or suffering.
"But why would the God of this Paradise order me out?"
They could smell sweet smells, unmatched and not com-
parable to any other smell. They rolled over each other, like
fish in a net.
"You don't know why he's ordering you out?"
They danced and sucked joyfully on each other. They
rolled in the grass and scattered cushions. As they climbed
trees, they acted as steps and ladders for each other. They
fell but did not get hurt.
"I don't know why he's throwing me out."
The desire they felt inside their tents and huts was unmatched. Lying down, standing tall.
"It's because you have been dreaming and thinking. For a
long time, you've been unhappy here."

"I don't believe that's why the Lord of Paradise is going to kick me out. It's not my fault if I'm miserable."

They were eating and drinking everything they craved and chose. Their glasses emptied and refilled, over and over. They had all day and all night.

"The God of this Paradise gets angry with people who think, dream, and feel sad in his Paradise."

"I don't believe the God of this Paradise is that harsh. He's lenient."

They ran, hid, and revealed themselves to each other. They swam, lay in the shade, swung, hid again, laughed and rejoiced.

"No, you're wrong. He's fair, but not lenient. Why would he want you in his Paradise, when no one here has touched you in a long time? For you, there is no morning and no night."

They don't think, read, or write. No dreams or pain. No worries or confusion. They're at peace.

"I once had a young man, more beautiful than any other."

They roasted birds and replenished themselves with fruit and fine pearls. They played with silk handkerchiefs and blossoming flowers. Woe unto anyone who stayed alone, who thought, dreamed, and became sad. They did not fight, envy, compete, or bear a grudge. They did not shy away from anything; for them everything was permissible.

"And why is that young man no longer with you? Don't you know that it's forbidden for a male to stay here without a female, as well as for a female to be without a male?

"I know that."

"So?"

"I've been unlucky since I came to this Paradise."

"We're sorry. Leave and go back to the land of misery."

She left, obedient and miserable.

"Get out! You can't stay here any longer."

He stared sadly at the guard. He recalled the happiness of this Paradise, which he had tasted for a while. He could see his misery materializing outside Paradise.

"But why do I have to leave here?"

They drank the unforbidden, ate whatever they desired, and sucked whatever they liked. They only finished their days to start their nights. They had all day and all night.

"Because ever since you've arrived here, you've been thinking, dreaming, and feeling sad. The God of this Paradise is expelling you as he has expelled others before you."

No alms or begging. They did not work or question. They had no memory and no regrets.

"I don't believe the God of this Paradise can be so cruel."

Parents and children were around the same age. Fine blond hair shone on beautiful legs, in a light that was neither daylight nor moonlight.

"You must believe and obey this command."

No envy or distress. They neither sin nor repent.

"I can't believe it, and I still don't understand at all."

They don't ask about their families or homelands. They don't remember who they were or where they are from. They have simply come, like those before them.

"I've never heard of what you're talking about."

From everywhere, they've come to this miniature Paradise in droves.

"I've come to you with what I know. You should not be questioning me about what the God of this Paradise ordains with regard to what he owns."

They were merciful to one another and shared what they owned with everyone.

"Is there no forgiveness?"

Origins and rank did not separate them. There were no differences in language or knowledge.

"In that regard I don't know any more than you."

They were comfortable as they lay there naked, the same way they had been resurrected. They were one another's mirrors and gifts.

"If only you would tell me a little of what you know."

"You spread boredom in people's souls. For you there's no morning or night."

"I had a girl, whom no other girl could match in beauty."

"But she's no longer with you. Who do you think will stay with you when you're so distracted? It's shameful to live here eternally without a partner."

"I realize that."

"So then . . . "

"I'm just unlucky."

He obeyed the order. He left, doomed by God's wrath. In front of the miniature Paradise's gate, the woman, ordered out before him, was waiting for her expelled partner. Their gazes met and their hands touched. They left together, in search of a new Paradise, one with no day and no night, no God and no guard.

Tangier, March 10, 1971

Upright Crawlers

The heat was intense. People who have exhausted themselves wandering about and chewing gum were breathing heavily. They yawned in sheer boredom. I was tired as well. I've been chewing my gum, weakly and wearily, for half an hour. Its taste made me sick. The city's many lights have just been turned on. They looked like hanging gardens. The city's main highway displayed the prettiest and ugliest things owned by its inhabitants and visitors. The fountain in the central square pissed its way along three channels, low, middle, and high, accompanied by rising and falling colors. The people standing around it were taking pictures of themselves, dazzled by the city's delights. Some of them were posing according to a photographer's instructions. I still had six pieces of gum, enough to last for three more hours of walking the city's streets.

I was stopped by an old, miserable, exhausted, and sick Moroccan woman.

"Give me gum, my son," she said in a weak voice.

The shops were crowded with people jostling to buy gum. Some were empty because they had run out of gum. A few poor young people were selling gum on the black market. I gave the old woman twenty francs.

"Buy yourself two packs," I told her.

She looked gratefully at the coin in the palm of her hand.

"Listen, my son," she said in a more begging tone. "If you've got any gum to give me, it would be better. I'm tired and sick. My throat's dry. And as you can see, the stores are crowded."

I was bored as I chewed my gum mechanically. The old woman kept pleading with me as she stared at my chewing mouth and exhausted, sleep-filled eyes.

"You can jostle with the others," she went on, "but I can't. I'm sick, my son."

She sounded desperate and sad. What she said was reasonable. I gave her a piece of gum. She snatched it and thanked me. I gave her another piece. She thanked me again and again, until I felt ashamed. I thought that if I gave her another piece, she would keep on thanking me—that if I kept on giving her pieces of gum, one after another, she would keep thanking me for each one until she fainted, went crazy, or died. I wished I had given her two pieces at once when she first asked. The exhausting effort that she was making in her miserable senility was causing me to despise this very existence and myself. I left her to work on the two pieces of gum and continued my wanderings, my slow, labored gait resembling that of all the other wanderers in this street and other streets as well.

I took another piece of gum out of my pocket and threw away the one I had been chewing. A homeless boy grabbed it, blew on it, cleaned it with his elbow, inspected it, and tossed it quickly into his mouth, as though he was scared that another child as miserable as he might grab it. I told him to take it out; I would give him a fresh piece. His eyes gleamed with both trepidation and anticipation. Another child just like him appeared and spoke to him eagerly, looking at me. Then they both looked at me, then at each other, then at me again, then at each other again. I watched them with a smile. The second child asked the first to give him a share of the gum he had been given. The first one took the sticky gum out of his mouth and looked at it. They both stared at me, smiling and afraid. I thought I would need to keep buying more and more gum until there was no more in my pocket, at the vendors or the market, or anywhere else, until I felt too weak to keep wandering this street and others.

A young woman hugged an iron electrical pole with her bare arms, wrapping her legs and arms around it. She kept spinning around it as she listened to a young man. She kept her eyes on him, on herself, on the pole, and on other men and things. A woman was sitting on a public bench with her back to the sea view, her eyes on the bicycles, while next to her a baby girl was sucking her fingers, which looked like a group of exhausted women. Three boys were standing there as well, looking like poorly stuffed sausages; they were eating a slice of red watermelon that they held by its ends. Dripping sugary juice, they passed it over their lips, smelling it as they licked it once with their tongues and then again, and taking it into their mouths as if they were kissing it. One young man offered his girl a big banana shaped like an erection.

"Here, take it," he said with a smile.

"Leave me alone, not now," she replied, smiling back.

They were both laughing as they heard brakes screeching, four wheels scrunching the road surface, in front of a little boy who was scurrying across the road.

"Here you are," he said.

"Not now. I already told you: Not now, later. Not now, later. Just as you wish."

Peeling the banana, he brought it up to his mouth and scraped it skillfully with his teeth, making it look like a penis. As the pair of them moved away with an easy laugh, the crawlers stood there upright. Cars collided. Women's cries were heard; a naked man ran by shouting wildly, chased by an even crazier man brandishing a large knife. A naked woman came out onto a balcony, screaming and pleading, "Suwailem, come back! Suwailem, leave him, come back, leave him alone!" Most of the people chasing the knife wielder were young men and boys. Near the building, gum chewers were gathering, coming together to chew their gum. The more they gathered, the more excitedly they chewed. I only had two pieces of gum left. What a mob! It was not so crowded in the shop across from me. Gum, gum, and more gum, before the crowds come back for gum and everything else.

August 1972

The Prophet's Sandals

More pleasure and fantasy, more money and tricks. Tired, tired—but I'm not satisfied. Fatin comes over, as white as snow in a blood-red box. She takes one of my notebooks and looks at me.

"Hey! My love!" she exclaims with a smile.

She is lost among those having sex with the air. Three o'clock in the morning. Boredom makes me nervous, while Umm Kulthum sings:

Sleep has never gotten anyone to live longer

Nor has staying up all night made anybody's life shorter.

A black customer comes up to me—whiteness on blackness. He takes one of my books and reads aloud: "This absolute freedom has its tragic and negative aspect . . . "

"What is this book about?" he asks, putting it aside.

"About a bastard who doesn't understand the world. He only bothers himself and those around him."

He shakes his head and lifts his glass to his mouth.

"You're stupid."

I notice Fatin writing something in a page of my notebook. I am drinking, smoking, and thinking about selling the Prophet's sandals. The electric power goes off. Women screaming. The lights come back on, and both women and men yell. I offer Rhimo another drink, celebrating the light being back on. She offers me her lips, and the sweetness melts in my mouth. Poking her brown tongue out, she chews the chocolate and tosses a red laugh. Fatin hands me the blue page.

"Rashid," I read, "do you know love? You talk about love more than you actually practice it. People who are ignorant of love find more happiness in it than those who know how it really is. Love isn't about knowing; it's a feeling, a feeling . . . !"

Miriam Makeba sings "Malaika" in her pure voice.

"Fatin," I write at the bottom of the blue sheet, "you're the red bed, and I'm your black bedspread. That's how I've come to understand love."

I'm looking for her: a foreign sailor is licking a scratch on her face, while she's hugging him with one hand and emptying her glass on the side with the other. Rhimo offers me her mulberries. I offer her another drink. More pleasure, more tricks and imagination. Melody after melody, voices reverberating as I think about selling the Prophet's sandals. Is it foolishness on his part, or confidence? Sometimes I have a hard time distinguishing the two. He's the one who made up that black myth. He wants . . .

She comes over to me, black, white, blonde. I offer her the blue page. For a moment, she looks at me and smiles.

"Hey!" she exclaims, "my love! My life!"

She takes the blue page.

She is a troublemaker, I tell myself. I look at her lips, so thin that they're like a healing wound.

For those dying of thirst, I am the dry lips: I recall the words of the Indian poet Mirza Ghalib.

She's searching for passion amid profound sadness. What I like about her is that she still believes that the world doesn't come to an end immediately after its creation.

Rhimo and Latifa are scrapping like two cats. Miriam Makeba is still singing in her pure voice as Rhimo grabs Latifa's black hair. She yanks her to the floor and kicks her in the face. Latifa screams as she bleeds. The colors blend together in my mind. Fatin puts the blue page down in front of me and goes over to join in the scrap.

"True," the blue sheet now reads, "I spread my flesh, but I don't feel I'm being raped. I long to be your death shroud in a tomb, with no prospect of resurrection."

Now Vigon is singing in a white voice: "Outside Window." Almond trees bloom in my mind, and snow stretches away to the distant horizon. I am behind the window, contemplating the void that has yet to be filled.

Rhimo and Latifa came out of the dressing room, now reconciled like children. They embrace each other and start laughing as they dance. I'm smoking, and in my imagination I keep slapping the faces of people who bother me. This one gets a kick, that one a slap, and the one over there a punch. This imaginary victory calms my nerves. Tomorrow I'll sell the Prophet's sandals.

"Why were Latifa and Rhimo scrapping?" I ask Fatin.

"Rhimo told the customer who was drinking with Latifa that she's infected."

"Is she?"

"Yes, but she says she's healed."

"This is the tastiest couscous I've ever had," the old Englishman said.

I looked at my grandmother, who lowered her head.

"It's Meccan couscous," I told him. "My grandmother's sister sends her some every month."

"Fantastic!" he said, giving me an approving look.

"Everything here in our apartment we bought from Mecca," I added, to stress the holy aura that envelops my grandmother. "Even this incense comes from Mecca with the couscous every month."

After he finished the couscous, the meat dish cooked with raisins and a mix of nutmeg, cinnamon, and cardamom was brought out.

"We call this dish mrouzia," I told him.

"Ah! Very good!" he said.

My grandma kept her head down modestly. The Englishman was eating the mrouzia, one eye on the food and the other devouring my grandma's face.

Her clothes were white, the incense gathered around her; smells of Arab perfumes and solemn silence. She had mastered her role the way I'd taught her.

The servant brought us tea, served on a small silver tray. Her clothes were white as well. She was shy, and she kept her head bowed. Clean, her hands painted in henna, her hair black and very shiny, her earrings large, her movements neat. She nodded to the Englishman without smiling, just as I had told her to do. The tinge of sadness on her face made her more beautiful than ever. The man let out a small ecstatic sound as he tasted the tea.

"Is it good, the mint tea?" I asked him.

"Oh! Yes, very good!"

The tea was perfumed with amber. There was a moment of silence.

Now comes that moment when Aladdin rubs his magic lamp, I thought. I got up and whispered in my grandmother's ear without really saying anything, just meaningless words. She shook her head without raising it. I lifted a white pillow and took out a green handkerchief embroidered with gold and white threads. The Englishman looked at the plain-colored sandals. He started stretching out his hand, then looked at me and understood from my expressions that it was forbidden to touch the sandals.

"My God! They're marvelous!"

I covered the sandals and gave him a chance to look at them through the pretty, transparent handkerchief. I turned around slowly and carefully, putting the pillow down as if I were applying a bandage to a wound. He gave me a quick glance and then took one final, long look at the sandals.

At Café Central, he nagged me once again—for the third time.

"So it's not possible?"

"It's very difficult," I told him. "It was hard enough persuading my grandmother to let you even see the sandals. Believe me, you're the first foreigner to see the Prophet's sandals. And believe me, no one else will see them but you."

"I understand that, but if you want, we can reach a deal."

"I understand, but what am I to do? The sandals are my grandmother's prized possession. If they disappear, she'll go crazy, possibly have a heart attack. I love her very much and respect her feelings about the sandals' holiness."

"I'll give you time to think about it. Try to persuade her."

"I understand, but persuading her to sell you the sandals

is a very different matter from persuading her to show them to you."

"Fine, but try to think of a way."

"I'll try, but I think it's impossible." Then, after a moment's pause I said: "Listen, there may be a way, but only on one condition."

"What?"

I hesitated.

"Speak," he said. "We can agree on anything. What?"

"That you leave Tangier as soon as I've handed you the sandals."

"Fine! A wonderful plan."

"I'm going to leave Tangier and go somewhere else. I won't be back until my grandmother dies."

"Fine! A wonderful plan."

"It will be impossible for me to stay here after the sandals disappear."

"I understand. I fully understand what you mean."

"Those sandals give her life."

"I understand. How much do you want?"

"A million francs."

"Oh! No. That is a huge amount."

"But you're buying the most beautiful historic artifact, and I'll remain full of remorse for the rest of my life."

"I know, I know. But that's a lot of money." He thought for a moment. "I'll give you half a million. I can't pay any more."

"You'll have to."

"I can't. I don't have that much money with me here."

"Fine, leave me your address. I'll write to you, and you can send me the rest."

We stared at each other in earnest.

Come on! Say it! I urged him in my mind. Say it quickly, Mr. Stewart!

"Okay. That'll work."

"Oh! That's wonderful, Mr. Stewart, wonderful!" I waited a moment, then asked, "Where shall we meet tomorrow?"

"I'll wait for you in the lobby of Hotel El Minzah."

"No. Outside the hotel. You have to have your travel ticket already when I hand you the sandals."

"Fine, understood."

"At what time?"

He thought a bit, still staring at me.

Make up your mind quickly, I thought.

"Three o'clock in the afternoon."

I got up and shook his hand.

"Don't tell anyone!"

"Of course. I know."

"The sandals don't just concern my grandmother, but everyone here who respects holy things."

"I understand."

I left. From a distance I turned around carefully and watched him get up and leave.

I found him waiting for me at the hotel entrance. As I approached him, I pretended to be worried. He looked excitedly at the bag in my hand. He was holding a package.

Half a million, I told myself. Yet more pleasure, more deception, fiction, and color.

I gestured to him to follow me and stopped at a distance from the hotel. We shook hands. He looked at my bag. I looked at his package. I opened the bag for him and let him touch the sandals for just a moment. He took the bag from my hand, while I took the package from him with my other hand. The corner of the package tore a bit.

"Half a million?" I verified.

"Half a million, yes," he assured me.

"And the address?"

"Oh, yes, I forgot. I apologize."

He took out a pen, and I held the package out so he could write his address on it.

"Now you'll leave Tangier," I stressed.

"That car's waiting to take me to the airport," he said, pointing to a car parked nearby.

And tonight, I told myself, I'll find myself in the Misa-lina pub.

I sat in my usual corner. I drank and smoked. I browsed the faces around me as I listened to the song "Honey, Honey." I was exhausted by pleasure—exhausted, but not satisfied. I can never be satisfied by just one woman.

"Rhimo is in the hospital and Latifa's at the police station," Fatin told me. "Rhimo was drunk and hit Latifa on the head with a beer bottle."

I asked her about two girls sitting in the corner opposite me.

"They're from Casablanca," she said.

I took one of my notebooks and walked toward the girls. I gestured at the younger one. She exchanged a few words with her friend. I was drinking, smoking, and waiting for the first kiss from a girl I had not touched before.

Her small face relaxed. Her mouth was like a strawberry.

I offered her a drink. She began to sip from the glass. Her lips glistened. Her lips cooled on mine.

Strawberries dipped in gin and tonic with lemon, I thought. Eve eating wild berries while Adam searches for her, lost. He moves close to her as she tries to eat the last mulberry before he embraces her. Adam eats the berry from her mouth. The berry inspires him to kiss Eve. Adam knows all the names, but it is Eve who has taught him the meaning of a kiss.

A couple of guys started fighting over a girl. The short one fell down, and the tall one kicked the air. Someone grabbed his arm from behind. Fatin placed the blue sheet in front of me. I was drinking, smoking, and sucking the fleshy berries from the mouth of new, young lips.

"I'm not who I was yesterday," I read on the blue sheet. "I know well what I'm unable to explain. You should understand me."

The small new face pointed at the empty glass. I looked at her mulberry mouth. The waiter amused himself by drawing boxes on a small piece of white paper.

"Give her another glass," I told him.

Her friend came over.

"Give her friend another glass too," I told him.

More berries and human flesh. More imagination and money.

"I must not understand you," I wrote on Fatin's blue sheet.

Tangier, November 1, 1972

Azrou

We entered the area around Azrou, "the Berbers' rocks."
Everything was cloaked in snow. Crows: the female delved
into the snow; the male embraced her, swinging on top of
her, spreading his wings.

"Pigeons fly happily when they finish copulating," Rashid said.

"Crows may be possessed by Satan's spirit."

"I see pigeons more often than crows."

The copulation took only a moment. I didn't know that
crows lived in the snow. Are they jealous of the pure whiteness, or do they come here to wash out the dust? We did not
see any other birds.

We arrived at Dayat Awa, and I asked what the name
meant.

"*Dayat* means lake," Moustafa explained, "and *awa* is either the howling of wolves or the name of a bird on its shores."

"I heard that Awa is the name of one of the lovers who
used to meet here, but they were forcibly separated. He died
of love, and she cried until she became blind and her magical tears formed this lake."

"That's what Rashid says."

We were driving through snow flurries and mist. The

road was deserted. Silent. The flurries looked like orchards of white flowers that blew onto the car's windows and then disappeared.

"My legs are freezing," Moustafa said.

"We'll drink some cognac when we get there."

The snow was getting thicker. The trees on our left were dense and covered in white. Whenever Moustafa accelerated, the wheels spun. He slowed down.

"They are putting gravel down in this area in particular," he said, "because of frequent car accidents."

Houses built of stone. Emaciated animals, using their snouts and hooves to dig into the rocky soil beneath the snow and find half-buried plants. Crows perched atop electrical poles. We heard caws. I could picture a white crow and pigeons possessed of the spirit of jubilation when they had finished copulating.

We saw a woman standing by her front door, arms crossed, staring into the distance. She was wearing a light-green dress. Her head was wrapped in a yellow scarf decorated in different colors.

"She's fighting the cold with those clothes," I said.

"They're used to it," Rashid replied. "I spent three years in Ifrane—it means 'caves' in Berber. I saw people walking barefoot in snow and rain."

Arriving, we parked the car in a muddy yard strewn with puddles and entered a small bar. In the middle of the room stood an old timber-fired heater. An elderly lady was serving at the bar, a brunette in unusual, brightly colored clothes. There was also a young man with fair skin. We asked for cognac.

"We have Rum Negrita," she said.

Between her intact teeth, which had not yet yellowed, were three gold ones. We ordered rum and coffee. The customers were subdued. They looked as though they had emerged from a coal mine and come straight here without washing. They examined us with probing looks. One of them ordered Ricard in an agitated voice.

"We're out of it," the lady replied calmly.

"You're only out because I've asked for it today!"

She showed him the bottle. There was not enough left to fill one of our small glasses.

"It doesn't matter," he replied, still aggravated. "Pour me whatever little is left and get me a beer."

She filled his order.

"I'm sorry," he said.

"It doesn't matter."

I went over to the hearth and took a seat. As I began to warm up, I took my shoes off and put my feet by the small door used when stoking the fire. Steam rose from my socks. Moustafa did the same. As we warmed ourselves, we drank up the last drops of our drinks. The other people there followed our every move.

"They were skinning us with their looks," I noted upon leaving the bar. "They don't like strangers."

"That's not true," Moustafa said. "You don't know them. They're brave and peaceable. We attracted their attention simply because we're strangers."

I asked about the place called "the landscape of Lalla Yatto."

"It isn't far from the city," Moustafa said, "but we'll freeze if we go to see it."

"I heard its legend once, but I don't remember it well."

"Lalla Yatto was a leader."

"A leader?"

"Her father was a leader. He resisted French colonization. He was a martyr, and she succeeded him."

"But Yatto the leader lived a long time ago."

"I'm talking about the Yatto from the French colonial era. It's said that they detained her along with her young son. When she refused to tell them where the resistance fighters' hideout was, they tortured her son in front of her. But she still wouldn't reveal the secret. Then they made her bleed between her thighs and cut off her breasts. Still she refused to reveal the secret. So they killed her, just as they'd killed her son before her."

"I heard they shot her," Rashid said, "and that she was a twenty-year-old virgin."

"I'd heard the story of Lalla Yatto the saint," I said. "She performed miracles. I also heard a story about her with a wolf and a peasant: she turned the peasant into a beast when he attacked the wolf."

We walked along muddy alleyways, their crumbling paths skirting grim houses with dilapidated walls. I could understand bits of what people were saying, since the words were similar to my own rural dialect.

We came upon a miserable child in tears, leaning against an old wall.

"What's wrong?" Rashid asked him.

The child looked at him, sobbing, but did not say anything.

"Leave him," I said. "He must be crying for bread."

"I wonder, when will the crying for bread end?"

"Not until the poor or rich all die off."

We returned to the square.

"We haven't seen any beautiful women yet," I remarked.

"They've been deformed by their useless history," Rashid said.

"The beautiful girls migrate to the cities, where there's more opportunity," Moustafa said.

We reached a neighborhood on the side of the mountain. Rashid asked a child about the district's name.

"This is a military base—so the Camp or the Barracks." He was carrying two plastic bottles. We asked him what was in them. "Water," he replied.

"You don't have water here?"

"Not yet. We bring it from the city. Only three houses here have running water."

He pointed toward a recently constructed house. "That's one of them," he said.

"What does its owner do?"

"He works in the power and water company."

He started walking again, turning on to another muddy path. The foothills were coated in snow. We arrived at the main square. For a moment we stared at the big rock overlooking the city, its edges blurred by snow flurries.

"In the summer, there's a small marketplace on top," Rashid said. "They go up there to enjoy the cool air."

On our return trip, we stopped in Ifrane. We had lunch in a well-heated restaurant. Rashid knew the owner, who was from Fez. At the far end of the room his two daughters were reading books, while their older brother, on vacation from school, was serving customers. The sky was stormy, and there were still snow flurries. Children raced each other over the thin layer of snow; scooping it up, they made snowballs and threw them at each other. We did not see any policemen.

"This is an ideal city," I told Rashid. "Its silence tempts one to live out one's days here."

"That's what I told myself when I first came here, but after a few weeks, I began to feel terribly lonely. Every weekend I'd travel to some other city. In winter, the city's dead, and in the summer it's taken over by people who never have to cry for bread. It's strange that I spent three years here without witnessing a single funeral. It's as though people here never die." He added, "Maybe they're buried quietly in secret."

Rashid took us to meet a family he knew. After a moment, he came out laughing.

"I found them all asleep," he said. "The oldest daughter woke up and opened the door for me, but I didn't let her disturb her mother and siblings. They're five orphans: three daughters—the oldest is around fifteen—and two older brothers."

"But it's six p.m.," Moustafa said.

"That's their habit at this time of day. They may also all wake up at two or three in the morning to eat something and then go back to sleep. When there's a disagreement between young and old, the younger ones can object. When a young person disagrees in a family meeting intended to hand out punishment, he'll be punished."

"And what do they live on?"

"The mother and brothers work, and the younger daughters study, but they've taken the eldest daughter out of school to take care of the household chores."

"Even in this town, then," I said, "there are poor people."

"You haven't seen the really poor people. They live outside the city boundary. They used to live in huts, but then they built them small houses so they don't spoil the city's beauty in the eyes of the wealthy."

We stopped in Imouzzer—a name that means "rabid" in one rural dialect, or "curly hair" in a different one. We went to the prostitutes' caves and found some of them standing outside.

It was very cold. They were wearing transparent nightgowns over wool sweaters and skirts or pants. Some of them invited us inside. We consulted. I refused, Rashid hesitated, and Moustafa insisted we go in to get an idea of how they live in their nests.

In the roof of each cave was a smoking chimney.

"The caves are heated," Moustafa told us. "Some may be well furnished."

The women's faces were daubed with makeup, their lips painted or dyed a cheap red, their hands covered with henna. Some of them had tattoos on their cheeks in the shape of small crosses. On most of them, the tattoos began at their chins and disappeared into their bosoms.

Is this an inherited religious tradition? I wondered.

"Let's go inside and drink some tea," Moustafa said.

"I'm not interested," I said. "There's nothing tempting here."

Young men were standing in the streets or wandering around, entering houses and caves. They either slowly left or remained loitering. Darkness began to shroud the place, and it turned a lot colder. From a distance passersby looked like ghosts.

We spoke to a woman who was standing at the doorstep of a recently constructed house.

"It's very cold."

"A bit," she said.

"When do you have music and songs?"

"Whenever you want; everything will be available."

"Are you by yourself or are there others?"

"I'm alone, but everyone will come."

She examined us calmly. We didn't say anything more.

"Come on let's leave," I said. "That's enough of this fooling around here. We're only doubling their misery. They must be cursing us because we're neither going in nor leaving."

"Are they good at sex?" Moustafa asked Rashid.

"If they're sober, they barely even take off their clothes. One of them will lift her dress and tell you, 'Go ahead, here I am.' But if they're drunk, they'll accept some flirting and foreplay, as happens in most worthwhile cities."

"Then they won't give head more than once at a time?" I asked.

"They haven't been broken in by sex yet."

We left the muddy street and went up some stairs to a café. A waiter was just leaving, and we asked if it was heated inside.

"Yes," he said. "Everything's available. I'll be back shortly."

Five women were sitting around a heater in the hallway relaxing. They were talking softly and smoking nervously. Two men were sitting in a corner. We asked for coffee. The waitress was beautiful in a natural way, but it looked as though she had never smiled in her life. She kept frowning at us as she brewed the coffee.

Why's she so hostile? I wondered.

One of the women went over and whispered to her.

"That ass is always late," the waitress said, "even if he's forced to work near the door."

It seemed to me as if she farted when she described the waiter as an ass. She plunked the cups in front of us.

"Let's just pay for the coffee and go," I whispered in Rashid's ear.

"Why? What's wrong with you?"

"Her coffee will make us sick, at least me."

"The people here are like that. They're good-hearted, but they don't do sweet talk."

"She makes farting sounds from her mouth."

We paid and thanked her. She looked at us as if she wanted to spit at us, as did the other women.

"What I've heard about the fun life in the cities we've visited is a big lie," I said to Rashid as we left the café.

"These women are miserable. We didn't invite even one of them to eat something with us. Their lives are barren, only fertilized by the occasional dirham."

A woman passed by, and we inspected her carefully. Her body spelled "prostitute" from top to bottom. Her smiling glance invited us back into the café we had just left. Meanwhile, Moustafa was busy opening the car trunk to make sure no one had robbed us. It was difficult to open.

"Something was jammed in the lock," he said.

"Let's leave before something worse happens," I said. "We'll try to fix it in Fez. I hate this useless region of Morocco."

"They don't steal here," Rashid said.

"What's this, then?"

"Children must have shoved something into the lock."

"But we haven't seen any children. Not even on the way into the city."

"They're children of the night. We don't see them, but they see us."

Tangier, February 1, 1980

Widows 1

It was a day like any other in her miserable life since her husband had been abducted. For months, she and her two daughters had eaten what was given to them by charity. Her husband had left her no inheritance or pension. She had been cut off from her family. She had not been able to find work in the city.

Originally she had been brought to the city from her village to work as a domestic servant for a family. Her employer got her pregnant, and she gave birth to two children, adding to the five he already had with his wife, the oldest of whom was thirty.

That morning she could not find even a scrap of tea to offer her two daughters, Amal and Nadia, as breakfast.

People in her village had never heard strange names like the ones she gave her two daughters. They called their daughters Fatima, Aisha or Awisha, Khadooj or Khadija, Rahma or Saadiya.

She was still young and beautiful, but men did not treat her with honor or respect.

The day was sweltering hot. She walked along the beach with Amal and Nadia bounding in front of her and behind her, playing with things they picked up from the sand. The fishermen were pulling their nets toward the beach.

For men, she thought, there are loads of professions. They can do many things for a living.

It had been years since she had felt warm sand under her feet like this. Also she had never before shed her clothes in the light of day and waded into the sea, as city women did. In the village she was not allowed to put anything but her feet, hands, or face in streams or rivers. Men were the only ones who could enjoy a river swim.

In front of her were lots of large, twisted rocks. Some of them were underwater, while others were only partly immersed. She clambered up to the top of a rock, looking for the best place to jump. Amal and Nadia both leapt into the vast, ebbing sea. She sat on the rock thinking about the fateful events that had made this the worst morning of her life. The rocks below were drowned in the surge. Small protrusions of rock breached the water, only to recede again. Would she jump alone, or with her daughters? She remembered the postman who would buy them candy or yogurt whenever he found them playing in front of the house. She liked him, but he had died in a car accident.

She noticed a fishing rod hooked to a hole in the rock, buzzing with flies. Between two small rocks was a crevice; in it were rancid fish and a jacket. Quickly, she climbed down from the rock and grabbed her children by their hands. She started walking hurriedly, imagining a monster's hand grabbing her from behind.

As she dragged her girls along, they could not keep up with her. One of them collapsed in tears. She stood her up again and pulled them along, but they kept crying.

At night, news of her despair spread among her neighbors, all as helpless as she. One after another, they came to offer her support. The image of that fishing rod, the rancid fish in the basket, and the jacket frightened her every time it resurfaced in her imagination.

Tangier, 1980

Widows 2

I washed and dressed them, and gave them breakfast. I had not yet had my own breakfast. I drank a cup of water. Broken-down beds: that was all that was left in the room. The only thing I had left to sell was my own body.

On my way down to the seashore, I used to look at the people and surroundings with neither affection nor sorrow. My two girls ran in front of me and behind me. I paid no attention to what they were doing. On the beach sand, the cool sea breeze eased my nausea and dizziness. Children were playing ball and swimming. Fishing boats were out on the water, and hooks, covered with tar, were embedded in the sand. On the shore lay the skull of an animal, deposited there by the breaking waves. I could view the situation with a clear mind, though my despair was powerful.

In the rocky area, I sat on a tall boulder that was removed from the ones covered by the waves. Tears overcame me. My two girls were playing in the sand and splashing in the water.

"What sin have her girls committed . . . ?" people will say about me.

A pile of clothes was lodged between two rocks nearby. I stopped by the pile of clothes: they were a man's, along with a hash pipe. In the gap between the rocks was a basket of foul-smelling fish.

I quickly made my way to my daughters. I grabbed them by the hand and briskly walked away. No one was there. As I was pulling them behind me, their legs buckled. They started crying and collapsed, while I, like a madwoman, kept looking back toward the rocky area. I stopped. My children sat on the sand, crying. I sat with them on the wet sand and fell asleep. I do not remember how I got home. That night I was struck down by a fever. My neighbor Tama brought me some soup. She stayed over, taking care of my daughters.

Next morning, all the neighborhood widows called on me, as did every desperate woman who knew me.

When I recovered, I thought of that man. Each time I used to pass by his store, he would flirt with me. As usual, I walked by warily. He came outside and invited me into his store to talk. I did not refuse. I knew what he wanted from me. If they had not kidnapped Hamid that night, I would not have gone into that man's store now.

Tangier, 1983

Aisha

When Aisha disappeared from our lives, it was extremely sad. Every evening, we would meet in Café Fuentes. She'd quit prostitution before she turned thirty, but she had aged prematurely. She was slim and pale, with crooked, rotten teeth—denied the perfect smile. She used to suppress her acid laughs by lowering her head to her chest. She started to work with Antonio, the café manager, as a waitress, then she became his mistress. There was nothing left in her to make him feel jealous, nor in him to make her jealous either. Not only that, but he also had gangrene in his leg, and that had aged him a lot. He used to spend the night moaning and groaning. Life's miseries bound them to each other.

His wife had died in Tangier and his children had married in Spain. They didn't think about him, except for occasional letters.

Fatima prostituted herself in order to have some money for daily expenses. She was waiting for someone to marry. She had lots of dreams, but did not talk about them. She bit her nails until she drew blood. She was young, stylish, and modest. She only spoke with her permanently smiling eyes; her voice was heard only when she was asking for or refusing something.

One day, Aisha bought a transistor radio. It delighted her to the point of obsession. In such miserable circumstances, she rarely bought anything new. Antonio might have bought it for her, or maybe she saved the money to buy it. No one asked her how she got it, and she did not say. A transistor radio was considered a luxury, especially among us, the poor. So we were drawn to her and her transistor radio. We touched it and inspected it as much as we liked. Even people passing by the café congratulated us on having a radio. We would ask Aisha to tune it to this or that station, and she'd respond happily to our wishes. She was the queen, and we were her guests. It was my impression that she'd never been as happy as she was that day.

That evening, Aliwa arrived, preoccupied and suffering from the effects of an entire day spent drinking. She ordered coffee and a glass of water and started cursing men. She had a bottle of vodka in her bag. We started to drink the vodka from a single glass, discreetly. Antonio and some café customers noticed us. They shared in our joyful celebrations, smiling from afar. I felt the fire in my chest and drank another shot. We did not dilute the vodka with anything else. That was what we usually did when we wanted to get high and drunk on just a small quantity of liquor.

Giving in to her intense delight, Aisha no longer pursed her lips when she smiled. That night, her decayed teeth were beautiful in their ugliness. When she laughed, she did not lower her head to her chest; instead, she raised her face, and her flat chest shook whenever she coughed. She lowered and raised the radio volume as she pleased, holding it close to her own ear, or to one of ours.

The bottle was emptied. Fatima left with a customer.

Aliwa took off too, half asleep and tottering. Next day we learned that she had quarreled with some security guards and they had taken her to a place where she would long for the sea that she loved so much.

Aisha lived with Antonio in a small house. She'd bring him food from the café. Every evening she would get home before him and wait for him to return so they could spend the night together. Usually, he would bring a bottle of wine with him. That evening, for the first time, Aisha begged me to walk her home because she was afraid to walk by herself. She was scared about the radio. She didn't say as much, but I could sense it. I could feel exhaustion weighing down my body. When I declined to escort her, she gave me a joyless good-bye. Once she had left, I felt so much remorse that I was on the point of dragging my body to catch up with her and walk her home or wherever she wanted.

Out of nostalgia, I took a tour round the old alleys in the neighborhood of Dar al-Barud. It had been years since I'd wandered there. I saw genuine renewal. From a small open window, Umm Kulthum's voice implored:

"Do you remember me, or have you forgotten?"

I remembered my childhood on the streets of Tétouan. Children in the small yard chasing one another. Desperate women and girls, noisily filling buckets with water from the public faucet.

I was standing under the window, sunk in my memories, when I heard:

"Choukri, what are you doing here?"

I looked up at the window. It was Bader. I hadn't seen him

in ages. A cord from above opened the door, and I went up. Neither of us had known where the other lived. We would meet in cafés in the Petit Socco or by chance at the homes of friends, staying late into the night. I had never seen him in the new city since I began living there.

I entered a small room. On its walls he had hung personal photos of his childhood and middle and old age, by himself, with someone else, or in a group. He was drinking tea, but he went and brought back an open, half-full bottle of wine and two small glasses. I noticed a framed mid-sized photo. My eyes opened wide: Aisha! Aisha at Bader's! How did he know her? Neither of them had mentioned the other, and I'd never seen him at Café Fuentes.

"Bader."

"Yes?"

"This photo."

"What about it?"

We raised our glasses in a toast.

"I don't know her," he went on. "A friend, Kennedy, brought it and left it here, then he immigrated to France. He worked in a canteen until he was shot."

"He was killed?"

"He quarreled with a Frenchman. They got into a fight. That same night, the Frenchman shot him."

"Would you give me the photo?"

"Since poor Kennedy's dead," he said, "you can have it if you want. Do you know her?"

"Yes. Her name's Aisha. She died more than twenty years ago."

"She has died as well? How?"

"She had just bought a transistor radio, and spent that

evening with us in Café Fuentes. On her way home, she was attacked by a drunken bum who wanted to steal the radio. She resisted him and hit him on the head with the radio. He broke a bottle of wine over her head, then stabbed her in the neck and chest."

He got up, went over to stand in front of the photo, and looked at it carefully, as if he were seeing it for the first time. Then he sat down.

"It's so easy for us poor folk to kill each other," he said.

When I was about to leave, I asked him again for the photo.

"I'd like to ask you to leave it here," he said, with genuine sadness. "Now it will remind me of poor Kennedy even more than it did before. He also lived poor in Tangier, and died poor in France."

The Tent

He grabbed my arm from behind.

"Here you are," he said. "Where're you headed?"

That is how my cheerful friend Abdun Furusu always surprises me. We walked along Samarin Street.

"Let's head for the Petit Socco," I suggested, "Khay Ahmed Bufrakesh restaurant. I haven't eaten anything today. All I had this morning was coffee with milk. I'm starving. But I don't have any money."

"So come with me then," he replied. "Let's go to Monopolio. There we can have food, drinks, and women. All our friends have tents there. They've got everything."

We drove through the outdoor market, heading for Bouabid Street. We passed the Dradab and Merkala. He dropped me off near the Boubana Christian Cemetery.

"You stay here," he told me. "Find some shade. I'll be back soon."

I watched his car climb Makraa' Road toward the Big Mountain. He must have a secret hashish smuggling operation up there, I thought. The time when friends trusted each other has died: that is what he always says. He's been in prison more than thirty times—mostly because he trusted friends. That is what Abdun Furusu and those like him who've been betrayed always say.

I sat under a willow, feeling refreshed and at ease. I love a summer night, relaxing beneath the branches of a tree by the sea. I thought about people from the time when Abdun was young: Anfolo, who was said to have head-butted a donkey one day, a head-butt that killed the beast—a feeble boy from the Saqqaya neighborhood used a dagger to remove its innards; Absaleemo al-Kundi, who was killed by Hamido Bodraa, using the knife with which he cut hash at a brothel in Bensharki; Dahesh, Kharat, Abu Harawa, Abu Tagine, and Abu Kradu, all of whom are drinking hard spirits these days—they doze on doorsteps and rummage through trash, companions to street cats and dogs. All the strong men in this blessed city fight with one other. Only in that way can they live and then die in their time. The people left behind live outside their time, killing themselves bit by bit, following their predecessors—either killing or being killed.

Still feeling refreshed and at ease under the tree, I saw in the dim light two figures approaching, their shadows swaying. They moved into the light of the moon and the streetlamps, then back again into the shadows of one tree, then another, over and over. They stopped and whispered, then moved toward me: two trees walking. They stared at me, like two hungry eagles. I felt cold, then hot, trapped under the tree. I leapt to my feet and stood there. They stared at me hungrily as they continued their slow approach. I could see claws peeking out from their sandals; their faces were dark. My wings were now weak, now strong. They stopped.

"Give us what you have!" the tall one barked. "Give us everything you have!"

"I don't have anything," I replied angrily. "We have food, drinks, and women—but only at Monopolio, where all our friends are."

I could hear my voice coming as if from a distance through the dark. I saw the color of night in their eyes. The tall one looked at the short one. The short one took out a shiny knife.

"We'll check to see if you have nothing at all," he said.

I was wearing a white sleeveless summer shirt, cheap wool pants that irritated my penis when it was erect. Even though it was midsummer, I was wearing those pants, as I had the summer before. My sandals were worn out and hurt my feet. I angrily removed my shirt and threw it at the cunning man. Then, just as angrily, I started ripping off my pants.

The tall one gestured with his hand for me to stop.

"Come and sit by me," he said. "Keep your pants on."

The short murderous fellow handed me my shirt. I screamed.

"No need to be afraid," the short one said. "There's nothing to be afraid of."

"The time of fear has ended. Now the time of hunger and plague has come."

I folded my thin shirt.

"Sit down," the short man said. "Don't let anyone see us."

I sat down, taking no comfort from my victory in defeat. True or not? It didn't matter, it really didn't matter. I felt like I was one of them. It didn't matter what happened. It was all the same, whatever happened, what will happen, at night or come daylight, with them or with others. I had defended myself.

We've all become equal, I thought—like teeth in a comb,

as the saying goes. Under this tree we're equal. True or false? It doesn't matter, it really doesn't matter. The dangers between us are the same, and so maybe thoughts are as well. I feel myself and I don't.

They both sat across from me. Everything's equal; nothing matters. The tall one took a bottle of wine out of his bag, along with a glass, black olives, and black cigarettes and matches.

"Where are you from?" he asked, clearing his throat.

"I don't have any money," I insisted, and went on: "We have food, drinks, and women. That's what Abdun Furusu told me. All our friends have tents at Monopolio. Our friends have everything, the entire world."

The two men looked at each other, bewildered.

"Let him go," the tall man told the short one. "Poor fellow, he's out of his mind."

He offered me a glass of wine, which I drank in one gulp, feeling thirsty and wild. They regarded each other again, still taken aback. I licked my lips and, with wide eyes, gave them as piercing a look as I could. The tall one handed me a cigarette.

"I don't have any money," I said again, firmly. "I don't have matches. We have food, drink, and women.

"All our friends are there at Monopolio," I went on. "They've got everything, the entire world."

I looked up into the branches of the tree, and they followed my gaze cautiously as well, as if waiting to see what would fall from it. In my imagination I laughed, with a smile then a frown.

I smoked greedily, and they watched, confused, almost

affectionate. I looked at the night and trees, then into their eyes.

"Put your shirt back on," the tall one told me gently.

I tossed it aside, spitting at it in the air. The short one went over and retrieved it from the spot where it had fallen. Calmly, I let him help me put it back on. The tall one offered me another glass of wine, and I gulped it down as fast as I had the first one. I laughed, and the short one laughed with me. We, the cunning, silly short one and I, laughed and laughed, while the tall one asked God to show mercy to his crazy servants. I felt relieved of my worries and fears. The tall one scolded the short one for laughing with me.

I've survived their attack, I told myself, and now they're protecting me.

I saw my friend Abdun Furusu's car stopping nearby, honking.

"Come on, Riffian," he shouted. "Let's go."

I leapt to my feet, grabbed the bottle, and drank straight from it, once, then again, and again.

"Take it easy," I heard the tall one saying. "You'll get drunk."

"What's going on there?" Abdun Furusu asked.

"Nothing at all, Mr. Abdun," the tall man replied respectfully. "Come and have some drinks with us. He's such a nice man, a fine one too."

They shook hands with me.

They must be from Tangier, I thought. They know who Abdun is. They probably know all our friends at Monopolio as well.

I laughed so loud that it upset the dogs. Laughing and

dancing, I made my way over to the car. The dogs were barking, at other dogs and at people. I opened the car door, and Abdun started asking me questions.

"What's going on with them?" Abdun asked. "Don't tell me you did your usual trick."

I got in next to him.

"Drive on, drive on," I whispered. "I'll tell you all about it."

We laughed a lot on the way. A bridal procession passed by us—cars packed with young girls clapping joyfully. They were playing wild music on drums and small tambourines. They were leaning out the car windows, reminding me of giraffes, and their arms moved elastically, like octopus tentacles.

"He's married her, married her," they yelled the words of a local wedding song. "He didn't leave her. She's married him, married him, and didn't leave him."

"We also have a wedding at Monopolio," Abdun Furusu said.

I was impressed by his new clothes: his shirt and pants were white and loose, his dirk tilted, with an ivory handle and a silver sheath, and his belt was black. He wore his black hair long, and his beard was black as well, with a few tufts of gray that made it more splendid; his eyes were dark, his teeth clean. The smell of his Arabian perfume refreshed me.

We arrived at Monopolio.

"Life is about food, drinks, and women," he said. "Till the plague gets to us."

We heard the sound of singing, chatter, and children crying. Women's voices, and dogs barking near and far. The stars, moon, and lamps lit up the tents, inside and outside. Wherever we looked, we saw signs of weddings. We walked along a pathway between the tents, hearing what was going on inside:

> Come, let us fill the gilded glass quickly
> Before it is filled by the hand of fate.

I remembered Nishapur, the Tigris and Euphrates, and the days of Sinbad. Ishtar killing her lovers, and Shahrayar killing the most beautiful women. Martyrs of Baghdad, throughout all times, hanged, crucified, burned, and buried alive.

"I saw someone drowning in the sea": a little girl's voice echoed from a tent.

"And in the sea," a little boy exclaimed, "fish will eat people."

"And people eat fish," the little girl replied.

"And people eat people in fish," the little boy said.

"You're an idiot," the little girl replied.

"And the feminine of idiot is idiota," the little boy said with a laugh.

Our feet slipped on pieces of wood, reeds, boxes, and tins. When one dog barked, others joined in, which encouraged sheep and other animals to add to the ruckus.

The voices of men and women were stilled.

"Kafur, shut up," a woman shouted at her dog. "May God bring you death!"

Someone threw something at the dog. It gave a sharp yelp and went silent.

I saw the loveliest thing: Abdun's tent encircled by those of our friends. By the entrance to the tall tent, a sleepy lamb lay ruminating; our arrival gave it a start. Inside the tent, reverberating voices welcomed us. The women ululated, celebrating how gorgeous Abdun looked. Zarifa al-Riffiya rose to hug and kiss him. Both were quivering with passion and delight. With intense longing, she tugged on his black hair, tinged with a delicate gray like almond blossoms at their brightest.

How wonderful to be in love, I thought, at the age of fifty, sixty, or any age!

She toyed with his shirt buttons, desire overflowing their passionate love for each other. She kissed his hairy chest as though she were biting him, while her hands clung to his ribcage and her belly hugged his. They seemed like one body with two backs. The softness with which she spoke was mingled with rebuke for the long time she had had to wait, tonight and other nights as well. It was as though all the love in her long life was just now awakening from a long sleep.

"I was about to put on my dress and go into the city," she said, "to wander the streets looking for you, wherever you were."

They laughed, and the love in their eyes was one of the most beautiful things I had ever seen.

"Leave me alone, you silly Riffian, leave me," he said. "I'm already drunk, and the night's still young. Go, take a swim, go . . ."

"Let's all go for a swim," she said.

He grabbed her cheek and stroked it gently. Her joy burst into words: "My flesh! My flesh! May God grant you death!" And then, fondly, she again suggested, "You and I, let's go for a swim. Let's swim. Let's all go for a swim."

Life's short, just a day, I thought. Being in love at the age of fifty or sixty is a whole set of lives. Afterward, we can welcome the plague.

We entered Abdun's tent. All our friends greeted us warmly. Hassouna lit two candles to mark our arrival and placed them on a black stone. One was large, a symbol for Abdun, and the other was small, like the rest of the candles on the black stone. I'm just his friend, and he's the link between me and those friends of his.

They were drinking, smoking, and jostling each other affectionately, taking pleasure in the wonderful music and singing. They had killed sadness a thousand times and prayed over its remains. Zarifa sat on the sofa, Abdun on a wooden box, and I sat on the floor, turning to look at the black stone. Mairubi offered us both wine. I drank some of my glass, then poured the rest over my head, asking for good luck and wishing the others long life. Everyone's voice was bursting with joy. I recalled the company of my comrades, the laughter and the good times in nights of old.

"What about the lamb?" Abdun asked Khay Ahmed al-Zahwani. "You haven't slaughtered it yet?"

"We were waiting for you," he said, "as supervisor."

Antar al-Sakouti got up and started sharpening a dirk against the black stone. I drank another glass of wine, ate black olives, and kissed Hassouna al-Manari, caressing her black hair.

"Life," I told her, "is nothing but this very life."

"Live, man," Abdun Furusu said. "Live, and we all live, man."

Their voices rang with joy. Hassouna picked up a kerosene lamp, and we all followed her, celebrating.

"Bring a bottle of wine," Abdun said to Zarifa, "so that we can pour it over the lamb,"

Khay Ahmed al-Zahwani and Abd al-Latif Donia held the animal's limbs firmly. The lamb, a terrified look in its eyes, stopped resisting.

"Baaa, baaaa, baaaaaa . . . ," it bleated.

The lamb gazed helplessly at the crowd. Eyes rolling, it started kicking. Antar al-Sakouti, the slaughterer, inspected his dirk, then rubbed it against his hand and his bare hairy arm.

"Baaaaaa, baaaaaa," the lamb bleated, suffocating and screaming.

Abdun took the bottle of wine from Darifa. Antar al-Sakouti checked the poor lamb's neck carefully, his mighty dagger in his hand.

"Houita!" Abdun Furusu exclaimed. "That is the new name for Zarifa al-Riffiya!"

"Baaaaaa," the lamb bleated.

"In the name of God the Almighty, for Houita," Antar said, the edge of the dirk shining in his hand.

He then killed the lamb with his dirk.

"Baaaaaa." The slaughtered lamb gave one final bleat.

The red fountain of blood kept on exploding; a mass of fat and two lumps of meat trembled and trembled, turning red, then white as the deep wound faded. The lamb's eyes glazed over, the fountain gradually ebbing. Delighted, Abdun Furusu poured the bottle of red wine over the lamb's throat.

"Houita! Houita! Houita!" we all yelled stupidly, monstrously, exuberantly.

We laughed and yelled, as the lamb still feebly kicked. Jenatha, Suleiman's companion, ululated in a throaty voice.

Abdun Furusu kept pouring wine on the dying lamb's throat, until Jenatha's young daughter, who had woken up in the other tent, came in with a bucket full of water.

"Shame, shame, shame, shame on all of you!" she screamed, tears in her eyes. "You slaughtered it at night and poured liquor on it. Shame, shame, shame, shame on all of you!"

With angry sobs, she splashed water on the dying lamb's throat to rid it of sins old and new. They carried the girl back to the small tent, to sleep next to her little sister.

The breeze now brought me the smell of the night sea. I hereby swear, by the death of this lamb, and the death of beloved ones, strong as bulls, that on such a night as this, life is turned into many lives, until humanity comes to its senses or the flood strikes.

We heard a woman screaming, somewhere far away from the tents. The friends all rushed in the direction of the screams.

The lamb keeps wallowing, shaking and bleating. As it does so, I'm breathing in the cool night air. Its limbs thrash in the air.

I did not want to rush toward the screaming like everyone else. I preferred to stay with the lamb in front of me as it gradually passed away and the red fountain slowed then stopped . . . Another sharp scream; children crying, women's and men's voices reverberating loudly—all of them echoing, including animals and nonliving things: stars, clouds passing in front of the moon, and the noises of the world all around me, old and new, beneath that night sky, between those tents, and the lamb, and this tent, and all those companions, brave as bulls.

"Life," Abdun would often say, "is nothing but the current moment, until the plague comes."

"Give me that knife!"

"Let go of that blade in your hand."

"Give me that big knife!"

Houita returned, breathless, dizzy, and sweaty. She stumbled over the ropes of the big tent.

"Gorilla's drunk," she said. "He's out to slaughter his girlfriend, Monica."

She went into the tent and rushed to the corner by the black stone, pleading with destiny, burying her face in her hands and weeping. She covered her face and pulled her hair, wailing and cursing. Then her hands relaxed, and her eyes grew cloudy as she sobbed, the black stone in front of me and behind her.

They came back to the tent. Gorilla was tottering; his face was scratched, his chest naked, his belly exposed. He was barefoot. Monica, half naked and barefoot as well, was drunk and crying. She was bleeding from her face, neck, and chest, her body covered with wounds.

Houita, now recovered, got up and hugged her friend Monica tightly. Hassouna al-Manari lit two more candles to welcome Gorilla and Monica and placed them on the black stone. We got them to stop wailing, to calm down and smile; then we had them consider the situation and, finally, laugh. We gave them whatever snacks they wanted.

Antar al-Sakouti and Abd al-Latif Donia stayed outside the tent, getting the lamb ready. Mina Saloumni helped them wash the body. Mairoubi served Gorilla a drink, the cup filled to the brim. His hand trembled, and a little spilled.

He drank it down in one gulp, though some of the red liquid splashed onto his bare, hairy chest, which was tattooed with women's faces, and with arrows and dirks penetrating a heart or two overlapping hearts. Tattooed words, some in Spanish, covered his body as well. He had gotten the tattoos during the forty-five times that he'd gone to jail, in the days when serving time was a source of pride and a mark of manhood in this city. His comrades had no fewer tattoos than he. "No one could be trusted. I love you very much, Jenatha," one said. "You're my love until death."

As we applauded, he stared at us with his protruding, hooded eyes. Abdun gave him a teasing shove on the shoulder, and again on his back and neck. Tugging on his hair, Abdun moved his hand down to Gorilla's chin. Meanwhile, Mamo tickled Gorilla all over his body, until finally he burst out laughing. He went outside to pee, then came back in.

We stopped the music of lost paradise, of old distant times, and started playing a song of invasion and loss in more recent times—when Tangier had gates that were closed at night and anyone trying to enter the city late would have to pay a fine, which was sometimes forgiven depending on how the guard was feeling or what status the latecomer enjoyed: "Oh, you Christian, the ship captain."

Mamo had the most beautiful voice. Gorilla started dancing, while we sang and clapped to the rhythm. He sang with us and clapped, placing his hands on his thighs and moving his butt right and left, drawing circles and half-circles in the air. Abdun Furusu took a fifty-dirham banknote from his pocket, wet it with his tongue, and stuck it on Gorilla's forehead. Gorilla's dancing grew even more frenzied. He was sweating hard; his face was red, his eyes teared with joy, and his lips were tight because he had few teeth. Mamo's voice was heavenly, and Gorilla's dancing was great.

We were done with singing, clapping, dancing, and crazy yelling, so, switching on the tape player, we started listening to old songs by Abdel Wahhab and Umm Kulthum. Some of them were relatively modern in their composition and performance, but they used classical words. Some were a mix of modern and classical, since some modern artists admire classical music.

"Give me your pussy," I said to Houita al-Riffiya in local slang, holding my full glass close to my mouth.

"Anytime."

"Now."

"Let's go for a swim."

"Would you give me your back?"

"My pussy I would give you," she said, laughing. "My back, I can't."

My eyes met hers, full of desire and lust.

"Come on," I said, "let's go to the sea."

"What's up, buddy?" Abdun Furusu asked, with his limited knowledge of the slang we were speaking. He drained his drink.

"Let's go swimming," I suggested. "Let's all go for a swim."

Houita walked ahead of us. Abdun and I followed her. We were both full of desire, our state of mind obvious enough as we touched, slapped, pinched, and caressed her dancing backside. Antar al-Sakouti was still slicing the lamb meat with a cleaver on a wooden box, while Mina Saloumni sat on another box, her glass in her hand. Donia was smoking hash and counting stars.

"Oh mother, what a night!" Houita declared to her friends. "Oh life, what a night!"

We heard a nursing baby crying inside a tent. A dog barked. The occupants of the tents celebrated with us, and we did the same in return. Dogs barked at the night, and at us. Insects chirred. Giggles could be heard inside many tents; in one tent the giggles were mixed with a song from Latin America:

Ay yay yay . . . sing but don't cry.
You were right, I swear, you're all I want,
she entered the garden, why, why, why.
And listen to the birds singing. Why are you looking at her?
Oh, you flower in my fantasy, I keep her in my heart,
like my father, no more patience with us . . .

All of the tents' occupants were singing and laughing.

Moving beyond the barking dogs, weddings, and insects' whistles, we raced like crazy toward the beach. I was behind Abdun, and Houita al-Riffiya was behind me. I purposely pretended to be in pain, so I could slow down and let Houita outpace me. I wanted to admire her body as she ran in front of me. I wanted to see her body from every angle. Abdun Furusu took off all his clothes and tossed them carelessly on the sand, then ran toward the sea, its surface a mosaic of colors. Houita did the same with her light clothes. In the shining moonlight, she appeared swarthy, except for her two half-moons, which were the color of dawn on a spring day. She was neither fat nor skinny, and had beautiful fine features. Shouting for sheer joy, she threw herself into the calm sea, which shone near and far like a carpet of light under the brisk night breeze. Whether naked or dressed, she had the perfect body, like her compatriots, mistresses of passion in the tents, in heaven or hell. Her way of thinking was neither entirely from the past nor from the present, though the larger part came from the past, with just a little from the present. Abdun Furusu is like that too, and so am I, along with the friends in the big tent and the many other tents. Like the two of them, I stripped and lay on the sand. I watched them immerse themselves in the sea and splash each other, squealing.

Right now, I thought, my entire world consists of those two there and me here. Nothing else exists but what's in front of me.

"It's enough for three naughty people to have a fun and worthwhile life," I said out loud.

"Come on!" Abdun Furusu urged Houita.

Laughing, running through the water, he chased and caught her, then let her go.

"No, no," she said. "Go on by yourself."

"Why, are you afraid? You chicken!"

"Yes, I'm a chicken. Go by yourself."

I watched her heading toward me, while he swam in the direction of the black flag, as powerful as a dolphin. I looked at my body. I was like a lamb, while my friends were like bulls. I did not have their jail experiences, or muscles suitable for tattoos and words of love.

She emerged from the water, walking slowly, showing off, contented and tired. My body was on fire from head to toe, and I shivered. An ecstatic fire ran through the veins of my penis, starting at the base and heading for the tip. Once it saw her pussy, it stood up saluting in respect.

"He's an idiot," she said, catching her breath. "He made

me drink sea water, and tried to drag me into the deep water so I'd drown."

My penis admired her wet, frizzy black hair. She lay beside me and lifted her lovely leg, the left one, a little. He trembled again, happily off-kilter. A throbbing desire overtook him, an intense desire. She looked at my penis, then at me, curiously.

"How many centimeters have you got there?" she asked jokingly.

"Twenty."

"Liar."

"Come measure it yourself if you want."

I flipped on my stomach and sucked her breast. She tasted sweet in my mouth.

That thing of yours is longer and wider than anything, I told myself. It's even more than twenty-five centimeters.

"Here's the sea," she said in the local slang. "Go drink from it till you've had enough."

"The sea salt on your skin is sugary," I replied.

I was not lying; her skin did taste sweet. Was it the sweetness of her skin in my mouth, or the sweetness of my mouth on her skin? I don't know. Maybe I thought it was sweet, so it became sweet. We laughed, and she lifted her left leg again. I was aroused.

"You are such a liar," she said.

"Your skin's the liar," I replied.

"What about my skin?" she asked.

I flipped on my back and saw Abdun Furusu standing on the diving board. When he moved, the sand came falling off him. He was fired up now, and he kept bending over, then straightening up again, arms flailing, as he prepared to dive. I thought about my own body, which wanted to jump and sink deep as well, the way Abdun Furusu was doing on the springboard, jumping and diving.

"You said it's twenty centimeters?" she asked

"I said come measure it yourself," I replied. "If you don't believe me."

She touched it, gripped it, first gently, then more firmly. She held it, then bowed and kissed it gently.

"Don't scare it," I said. "Let it swim or leave it alone."

She looked at the boats by the shore, then at it, and got up.

"Come on, then," she said. "Let's see what this twenty-centimeter thing is all about."

I knew that Abdun Furusu never got jealous over a woman. To him, all women are the same. They're all one woman, and one woman is all women. He liked Abderrahman al-Majdoub's verses:

> The hat flew and fell on the waterlogged wood;
> Every woman is a whore except the one that is not capable
>   of anything.

Being over fifty, his two wives were enough to satisfy him once in a while. He never forced me to do anything I could not do. On celebratory occasions he had often left me women and presents, at the tents, at my own house, or at generous friends' houses. For him, satisfaction lies in offering pleasure to me and other poor friends.

"Time spent suffering and wasting dignity over a woman is not worth it," he'd told me one day. "It's best to think only about those who think about you."

I followed her as she walked, skipped, and ran. I was right behind her, and if she flew, then fell and got up, so did

I. When she bent over, I did the same. We raced to the water and rinsed the sand from our bodies, cavorting like children. She rubbed me, and I rubbed her. Like children, we sneaked our way among the fishing boats and across the sand at the water's edge. I felt cold and hot, I on top of Houita, and she on top of me, between flesh and sand. We stayed long enough to melt some fat and sweat. We were both relaxed, satisfied, and content, looking toward the festival in the sky.

"You're stronger than Abdun Furusu." she said, "in both fornication and imagination."

"But his arm is stronger than my entire thigh," I replied.

"That doesn't matter," she said. "Your thing is long and strong; his is short and weak."

"But he's over fifty," I explained, "and I'm not yet forty."

"You beat me, damn you!" we heard Abdun yell. "You played your game with her before me. You bastard, you had her before I did!"

"The only people you should think about," she said with a laugh, "are the ones who think about you."

"You've beaten me with my own sword, damn you!"

All three of us raced to the water, laughing, jumping, and playing like children. The water was cold here, then warm, like Houita's vagina. I felt cold and hot under the tree, on top of Houita and underneath her. Between flesh, sand, and sweat, the smell of fish in wood and seaweed, above and below the water, in the air that night, beneath that sky.

Our friends appeared, cheering and roaring like bulls. We watched them behaving like us. Life is nothing but cold and heat, until, as Abdun Furusu says, the plague and flood come.

Tangier, March 8, 1973

Translator's Acknowledgments

As I write these words, it has been almost eighteen years since the passing of the Moroccan author Mohamed Choukri. He left behind many unparalleled literary works that the typical reader of English has never seen before, much less read. This text brings some of his stories to light.

It took many long months to experience Choukri's words, to breathe them in and linger in their riches, before I could bring them to English readers. I remain deeply indebted to a host of friends and colleagues whose support was immensely helpful. Although mere words cannot truly convey my gratitude, they will have to do.

I'd like to thank Roger Allen for his extraordinary assistance with this book. He read the entire manuscript more than once and offered excellent suggestions and corrections. The same goes for Kelly DeLuca, Karl F. Otto, Jr., and Afaf Tamim. Their comments were insightful and challenged me to take a different look at the translation; for that I am in their debt.

Appreciation and gratitude go also to Hanan Badawi and Luke Leafgren, as well as to Alicia Ayers, Kirstin Bratt, Susan Chenard, Nour El-Kebbi, Laura Hope-Gill, Adriana Jacobs, and Chris Malley.

With regard to permissions, I would like to thank my dear friend Najoua Fathi for her Herculean efforts to find the holders of the rights to these stories, thus helping me to secure the permission to publish. She made several trips to Tétouan and Tangier, and in the summer of 2019 she introduced me to the family of Mohamed Choukri, who welcomed me and helped smooth the permissions process. In particular, Tarek Choukri, the author's nephew, has shown great interest in the project and offered unwavering support. I'd also like to thank Abdellatif Benyahya, former director of the Mohamed Choukri Foundation, for sharing with me some personal anecdotes about the author, and for his invitation to the Tangier Summer Festival in 2019, which gave me a chance to speak about this project and to see the city of Tangier through Choukri's eyes. Experiencing specific places in person was a tremendous help as I worked to translate the stories.

I have had the good fortune to work with Yale University Press. Members of the staff, in particular John Donatich, Danielle D'Orlando, Ash Lago, Susan Laity, Kristy Leonard, Sarah Miller, and Abbie Storch, have been most professional and made this process very smooth. I am also grateful to the anonymous reviewers for their suggestions and feedback. Their input has enriched this work.

As with any translation, the task of rendering these stories into English has been both challenging and rewarding. My main goal has been to allow English readers to experience the same joy I feel every time I read Mohamed Choukri. My hope is that everyone reading these stories begins to be more curious about the literature and the culture from which they spring. These stories speak to me, and I am delighted to share with you this labor of love.

MOHAMED CHOUKRI (1935–2003) was a key figure in twentieth-century Arabic literature. Born in Morocco, he is best known for his autobiographical novel *For Bread Alone*, which was translated into English in 1973 by Paul Bowles. The book was censored in Morocco from 1983 to 2000, but it has since been translated into more than thirty additional languages. Choukri grew up in the Rif mountains and then in Tangier, and he did not learn to read and write until the age of twenty. In addition to the stories in this volume, his other works include autobiographical novels, a play, a book of essays, and numerous accounts of his time spent with foreign writers.

JONAS ELBOUSTY holds M.Phil. and Ph.D. degrees from Columbia University. He teaches in the Department of Near Eastern Languages and Civilizations at Yale University, where he served as director of undergraduate studies for six years. He is currently director of undergraduate studies for the Modern Middle East major, and he also directs the Arabic Summer Study Abroad Program. He is co-editor of *Vitality and Dynamism: Interstitial Dialogues of Language, Politics, and Religion in Morocco's Literary Tradition* (2014), co-author of *Advanced Arabic Literary Reader* (2016), and author of *Media Arabic: Journalistic Discourse for Advanced Students of Arabic* (2022) and *Aswat Muasira* (2023).

ROGER ALLEN is Sascha Jane Patterson Harvie Professor Emeritus of Social Thought and Comparative Ethics, as well as Professor Emeritus of Arabic and Comparative Literature, at the University of Pennsylvania.